THE LYON'S LAIRD

The Lyon's Den Connected World

Hildie McQueen

Dragonblade Publishing, Inc. is an imprint of Kathryn Le Veque Novels, Inc.
P.O. Box 7968
La Verne CA 91750
ceo@dragonbladepublishing.com

Produced in the United States of America

First Edition May 2020
Print Edition

ARE YOU SIGNED UP FOR DRAGONBLADE'S BLOG?

You'll get the latest news and information on exclusive giveaways, exclusive excerpts, coming releases, sales, free books, cover reveals and more.

Check out our complete list of authors, too!

No spam, no junk. That's a promise!

Sign Up Here

www.dragonbladepublishing.com

Dearest Reader;

Thank you for your support of a small press. At Dragonblade Publishing, we strive to bring you the highest quality Historical Romance from the some of the best authors in the business. Without your support, there is no 'us', so we sincerely hope you adore these stories and find some new favorite authors along the way.

Happy Reading!

CEO, Dragonblade Publishing

Additional Dragonblade books by Author Hildie McQueen

Clan Ross Series
A Heartless Laird

A Hardened Warrior

A Hellish Highlander

The Lyon's Den Connected World
The Lyon's Laird

CHAPTER ONE

E VANGELINE PRESCOTT HAD become used to the confines of her beautiful home, a gilded cage one could say.

She'd transformed her bedroom into a haven. Books stacked on surfaces, vases with flowers she personally picked from the garden and her lazy, orange cat, Lucille, made for a perfect sanctuary. If only she could remain there forever, curled up on the window seat rereading her favorite books while occasionally peering out the window to the street below.

A carriage rumbled by. The manner in which the horses pranced seemed to indicate they enjoyed the perfect weather on that particular spring day.

For a moment, she imagined riding in the carriage, contemplating where she'd choose to go. With a frown and a shake of her head, Evangeline realized there wasn't anywhere she'd prefer to be than at home.

While others of her social status would consider her life a sad situation, she couldn't imagine why. After all, her life was complete. She had a close friend. Her father and mother doted upon her. And if not for the certain imperfection and an unfortunate incident, her life would be perfect.

Just then, a black carriage with a familiar emblem came to a stop at the front gates of her home. The driver peered up to the house before climbing down to assist his passengers out.

"Oh, no," Evangeline grumbled, which made her cat, Lucille, lift its head, its luminescent green eyes scanning the room. The cat, used to her outbursts, lowered its head back to the cushion and closed its eyes.

Outside, a younger woman exited the carriage, dressed in a blue morning gown. She daintily took two steps to the side so that her mother, who wore a much too bright shade of yellow for someone her age, could join her.

A family footman promptly opened the gate to allow the women in and Evangeline leaned back as they disappeared. Since she'd already made an appearance at breakfast and had announced she planned to enjoy the beautiful day in the garden later, it would be impossible to feign illness.

It was but a few moments before the knock on the door meant she could not hide any longer.

"Yes?" Evangeline called out, remaining hopeful that perhaps the maid would bring a message to remain upstairs.

A maid named Fran pushed the door open and walked in. "Miss Evangeline, your mother requests that you come down. Your aunt, Lady Monroe, and her daughter, Prudence, are here."

"Very well." Evangeline closed her book and placed it on the bench beside where she was sitting. "Tell her I'll be down momentarily."

ONE STAIR AT a time, Evangeline ensured her footing, doing her best to ignore the gazes that followed her progress. Despite her mother continuing the conversation, Lady Monroe and her daughter did not tear their gazes away from Evangeline. Even when she finally took the final step and made her way to the settee, the older woman continued to stare.

"My goodness," her aunt said after Evangeline greeted her. "I certainly thought the last treatment would provide some kind of improvement to your leg. But you are still as encumbered. Your limp is quite pronounced."

"Perhaps she will remain that way," Prudence added, her wide eyes meeting Evangeline's with feigned innocence.

How her mother and this woman could be sisters perplexed Evangeline.

The sisters were complete opposites. Her mother was blonde, beautiful and kind, while her aunt had dark brown hair and a permanent crease between her brows as she was permanently displeased about everything.

"She is doing much better." Evangeline's mother attempted to smile, but it was evident to Evangeline that she was not pleased with Lady Monroe's rude comment. "We have decided to allow Evangeline a respite from any more treatments."

"I suppose one can only do so much," her aunt replied.

Evangeline gave her aunt a bland look. "I am so very grateful you care so much about my treatments, Auntie."

Put in her place, her aunt turned to the doorway. "Is tea being brought all the way from China?"

"The spring social season is upon us. Isn't it exciting?" Prudence said with overly exaggerated glee. "We came to deliver an invitation in person. They are so very lovely," Prudence gushed. "You will be a dear and help me with the flower arrangements again this year, won't you?"

For the last several years, the Monroes hosted the first ball of the season. And every time, they would invite Evangeline to be part of the planning. Which was a nice gesture on their part, while at the same time a stark reminder of how excluded she was from other social gatherings.

Due to the unfortunate incident, she never received an invitation to more than tea at some houses which, in and of itself, was rare.

As much as Evangeline hated social occasions, she loved being part of transforming a stark ballroom to a beautiful oasis. And she would always help, even though Prudence was annoying. She treated Evangeline with as much disdain as any other person.

"Of course, I will help, although I am not sure I'll remain for the ball itself."

Prudence gave her a knowing look. "You can sit and enjoy the music. It will be nice to see what everyone wears. I am sure your friend, Rose, will join you as she never has an escort either."

"That's true. There will be plenty of chairs available for both of you. Unlike you, Prudence cannot sit about," Lady Monroe interjected, her lips curving to a smile that did not reach her eyes. "As hostess, Prudence will be required to entertain and dance. This is the year we will strive to find a proper match for a marriage for her."

"The invitations have gone out to a group of rather promising gentlemen," Prudence informed them. "One in particular, I hope to get to know better."

"Who is that dear?" Evangeline's mother asked.

"I prefer to keep it to myself for now," Prudence replied, inspecting her nails. "He is the talk of the town, however."

"There are plenty of eligible men, even some outside our circles," Evangeline said. "There are shop owners. Why, the owner of The Tattered Page is single…"

"A bookshop owner?" Lady Monroe held her hand to her chest. "Honestly, Olivia, you should worry about your daughter's choices."

Prudence wasn't necessarily pretty but she did have lush, brown, wavy hair that was often remarked upon. Her suitors often lost interest once they were subjected to her constant pouting and complaining.

Tea was brought and placed in front of Evangeline's mother and she poured for everyone. Her hand shook, but she poured without incident, ensuring to place an embroidered doily under each cup before passing it to the others.

Just then, there was a knock at the door and Evangeline's friend, Rose Edwards, was announced.

Dressed in a beautiful green morning gown, her auburn hair pulled up into a simple style, a happy Rose walked into the room. The bright smile faded at noting Lady Monroe and Prudence were in attendance.

Rose's bright blue eyes met Evangeline's. "Oh, I am so sorry. I didn't mean to intrude." She curtsied in front of Lady Monroe. "Pleasure to see you, Lady Monroe and Prudence."

Her aunt barely acknowledged Rose.

"Nonsense, you are quite welcome, dear." Evangeline's mother motioned to an empty chair. "We are discussing the upcoming social season and your perspective would be greatly appreciated."

Lady Monroe blew out a breath. "Yes, well, I am sure my Prudence has plenty of knowledge of what is popular this season. She has already attended two social gatherings and several teas." Her eyes slid past Evangeline to Rose. "How many have you attended?"

Rose blushed and shrugged. "Evangeline and I went to a tea just yesterday. It was most delightful to spend time with Lady Turlington."

Both the Prescott and Edwards families had always enjoyed spending time with the older, eccentric Lady Turlington and her husband. Although titled, the duke and wife rarely left their home. With only one son, they rarely had company and so Evangeline, Rose and their parents often visited the old couple.

The Edwards family was not as connected to social circles as the Monroes. Rose's father owned Arthington's, a high-end furniture store. The family fortune came from sales and not inheritance like that of well-established families.

Like most titled men, Lord Monroe, Prudence's father, had not earned any of the money the family boasted about. They lived from the family fortune left from generations before.

Evangeline smiled warmly when accepting the tea from her mother and then turned to Rose. "Prudence has invited me to help with the décor of the ballroom again this year."

"Delightful," Rose replied in a rather bland tone that made Evangeline struggle not to laugh.

Prudence was, of course, oblivious met Rose's gaze. "You can help as well. I am not good with the menial tasks of plopping flowers into vases."

This time, Evangeline giggled. "We will certainly help."

Her aunt and Prudence began discussing the upcoming season's plans with her mother which, of course, did not include Evangeline.

"Should we discuss the next meeting of the book club?" Evangeline asked Rose.

For several years, they and three other women had formed a small but vibrant book club that met at The Tattered Page, a local bookshop two blocks from Hyde Park. The gatherings were a weekly highlight for Evangeline, who rarely ventured out.

Jarod Tuttle, the owner of The Tattered Page, was a rather awkward man in his late thirties. He was another reason she and the other ladies looked forward to the meetings. Despite his shyness, he was attractive and attentive to their group. He never criticized their choice of books, which made him acceptably forward-thinking in their eyes. They'd all harbored light crushes on Jarod over time.

"IT'S SAD THAT I am grateful when my sister leaves," her mother said later that day after the three women left. "I must admit to secretly wishing she would move to the country like they've been considering."

Evangeline laughed. "My aunt considers you not only a sister, but a friend. The poor thing doesn't realize she has none."

Her mother's lips twitched. "I know." She let out a sigh. "My trembling gets worse whenever she's around, which seems to give her glee."

"The doctor does advise that you avoid stressful situations." Evangeline studied her mother's hands, which were still at the moment.

Evangeline stood and went to the doorway. "I will oversee dinner preparations. Let's pray that Father's business associate who is joining us is pleasant." She met her mother's warm gaze. "Remain here and rest."

Her mother reclined against the pale-yellow upholstery of the sofa and lifted the teacup to her mouth. "Thank you, darling."

Through the windowpanes, sunlight filled the room, giving it a beautiful glow. Evangeline fought the urge to go to the tall windows and peer out. Prone to daydreaming, she could stand at the doorway to their garden for hours and not realize the passage of time.

Down the short corridor and past the dining room, Evangeline made her way to the kitchen. Just as she entered, Martha, the cook and head housekeeper, hurried from the table in the center of the room to look into a pot.

"It smells delicious," Evangeline proclaimed.

"If it doesn't burn first," Martha replied, giving the young maid, Fran, a stern look. "See about chopping the rest of the carrots," she instructed.

Fran gave Evangeline a bright smile. "Miss Genie, did you go out to the garden yet? It's a beautiful day."

"Not yet," Evangeline replied. "You're welcome to come with me when I do go."

Martha cleared her throat. "Fran most certainly will not go about the garden. She has much to do. Remember your place, Fran."

"I'm sure it's fine for us to…" Evangeline started.

"No, it is not, Miss Genie," the older woman said, also using her family nickname, which made Evangeline want to laugh. "Your mother has corrected both of you on plenty of occasions about all this frolicking."

Evangeline winked at Fran before looking to Martha. "Mother is resting, so I came to ensure you are made aware we will have a guest tonight. A gentleman."

"Very well, Miss. I will ensure everything is just right." When Martha turned her attention back to the meal preparation and Fran began chopping, Evangeline strolled back out of the room.

The dining room was not as ornate as other homes she'd visited, as her mother preferred understated décor. The walls were a soft gray with square off-white inlayed wainscoting around the room. Centered in the space was a rectangle mahogany table with four chairs on each side and two on the ends. The only décor on the table was an over-sized vase that spilled over with flowers and thin branches that had been expertly arranged by her mother.

Perfectly centered over the table was a sparkling crystal chandelier.

Evangeline walked around the perimeter of the room with a critical eye. She inspected the surfaces of the sideboards and the two red upholstered settees that were positioned across from each other against walls. Everything was acceptable for company. The only tasks left were to instruct the table be set with the blue china and the new set of crystal goblets her father had acquired during a brief trip to Austria.

Just then, Fran walked in carrying a tray upon which were folded napkins and silverware.

"Perfect timing," Evangeline said and continued on with instructions to Fran as to which items were to be used. Once she was assured the young maid understood what was expected, she decided a walk alone in the garden was warranted.

As if her cat had some sort of mind reading ability, Lucille raced past and stood next to the set of French doors. She meowed softly and rubbed against the door to make her point clear.

"Very well, I will allow you outside, but only for a short while." Evangeline opened the doors and the cat sprinted out.

In the garden, she walked to a flowering bush and considered trimming blooms for her bedroom. The day was, indeed, lovely. The sun was warm, but not too much so and there was just enough of a breeze to ensure comfort. Birdsong filled the air as Evangeline made her way to a bench.

From where she stood, Evangeline had a clear view through the doors into the sitting room where her mother continued to lounge. There was something strange about the way her mother was acting. Not just during the Monroes' visit, but since the day before. It was as if there were something weighing heavily on her mind. Evangeline narrowed her eyes. Or her mother was up to something. Although she knew her mother wished for her to marry, it actually happening was doubtful.

After dinner and the visitor left, she would sit with her mother and have a talk. There was nothing to be worried about as far as Evangeline was concerned. The family finances were in order. As a matter of fact, apart from her father's accounting business, her mother was quite wealthy in her own right.

Upon marrying Forest Prescott, Olivia Murray Prescott had brought with her a large estate and other property holdings. Not only that, but Evangeline's bank account held a grand sum left to her by her grandmother.

Despite her family's wealth, they lived a simple life. The household staff was smaller than others in their same social status and although the London home was beautiful, it was not grand.

Evangeline had one sibling, an older sister, Priscilla, who lived at her mother's country estate near Manchester. Although out of the city, it suited her sister and husband perfectly as he preferred to spend his days out with his horses and she loved to garden.

The other Prescott family home, a beautiful sprawling country home was also near Manchester, was where Evangeline and her parents spent several months out of the year. Although it was a nice respite from the city, Evangeline did not prefer it. She loved the activity of the city and enjoyed her book club too much to miss it for long periods.

By THE TIME her father arrived that evening, along with the dinner guest, everything was prepared and ready for dinner.

Her father introduced Evangeline and her mother to the man, who looked to be in his early forties. Mortimer Witt was a business associate, her father explained as they made their way to the dining room. Apparently, the man was investing heavily in a company that he wished her father to investigate.

The man took an extra-long study of Evangeline once they were seated until she fought not to fidget.

"Mister Witt," her mother said, thankfully taking his attention. "Are you a native Londoner?"

After glancing at her mother, the man looked once again to Evangeline. "No, I spend most of my time south of here in Hertford-shire. I come to London to conduct business but find the city much too," he hesitated before finishing, "filthy for my liking."

"I agree it is crowded, but I would not describe London in such a manner," Evangeline said, not at all liking the man.

Her father gave her a stern look and added, "There are some beautiful sites here."

"I do not mean to offend you," Mortimer said in a soothing voice that, for some reason, made Evangeline's skin crawl. "It is just that the country is so much more pristine compared to the city streets."

Annoyed now, Evangeline turned to her father. "We should invite Mr. Witt to help with the cleaning of the stables and pig sties at our country estate. That is not what I'd call pristine."

"Evangeline!" Her mother's wide eyes moved from her to the visitor. "I apologize. My daughter has had a trying day."

"No need." The man had the audacity to smile at her. "I like women who are not afraid to express their opinions."

Thankfully, her father intervened and the two began to discuss the financial standings of London businesses. It left Evangeline and her mother to offer an occasional nod or acknowledgement of whether or not they'd heard of said business.

Dinner took an extraordinary long time since Mortimer spoke in between each and every bite.

When fresh fruit compote was presented, the visitor was delighted to try it. Once again, the conversation continued as he ate each piece of fruit separately.

Several times over the meal, his gaze moved to her and Evangeline pretended not to notice. Better to avoid than to offend as she didn't wish to compromise her father's business in any manner by being rude and glaring back at him.

Thankfully, once the meal ended and the man left, she'd never see him again. Of course, she'd beg her father never to invite him again.

When dinner was completed, as was customary, her father invited Mr. Witt to his study for an aperitif, which suited Evangeline perfectly as she didn't wish to remain in the man's presence.

"That was a long meal," Evangeline pronounced when she and her mother entered the salon. "Mr. Witt seems to savor every bite of food."

There was a deep crease between her mother's brows. "I will admit he is a bit strange."

"Did you notice how he stared at me? It was quite rude." Evangeline poured sherry into dainty crystal glasses.

Her mother accepted the glass. "Your father had another reason for bringing Mr. Witt here for dinner, Evangeline. We have discussed your situation and have decided to find a husband for you. It is time to consider having a family of your own."

"Absolutely not," Evangeline exclaimed and got to her feet. "That man makes my skin crawl."

Her mother stood and rushed to the pocket doors of the salon and pulled them closed with swiftness. "For goodness' sake, keep your voice down." She shook her head and blew out a breath. "You are much too outspoken."

"Why would Papa think Mr. Witt is suitable," Evangeline whispered. "He doesn't care for London and was…"

"I know, darling. Don't worry, I've been fretting over this and may have a plan to get you married to someone more agreeable."

Evangeline let out a long breath. "Whatever it is, disregard it."

Taking Evangeline by the hands, her mother led her back to sit. "I have a good plan. You will marry someone that is more pleasing and the choice of man will be much better. I am assured you will be well pleased."

"What are you planning to do, Mother? I am well, you know, not physically perfect in the least. Most men prefer a woman who is able-bodied."

Olivia Prescott shook her head and huffed. "Not only are you beautiful but you are more than able to perform the task of running a household. Other than your slight limp, I don't see what a man could find lacking."

Her leg ached, a reminder of the last set of excruciating treatments.

The doctors had not only not helped her limp but now there were recurring twinges that hurt.

"Very well, Mum. I am willing to listen to whatever you have planned. But rather than marry an unpleasant man like the one in Father's study, I will prefer to remain a spinster."

"You are not a spinster," her mother said in a rather unconvincing tone.

Evangeline smiled. "Mother, in two years I will be thirty. I have been a spinster for several years now."

There was an interesting combination of determination and pride as her mother met her gaze.

"Do not fret, darling. Tomorrow, I have a very important woman to meet. All will be well."

Her mother's words sounded more like a warning than a statement meant to soothe.

CHAPTER TWO

C AMREN MACLEAN STRETCHED his long legs, heels crossed on a footstool, a glass of whisky held lazily in his right hand as he listened. Gideon Sutherland, who'd traveled with him from Scotland, stood by the hearth. He, too, held a glass of whisky, which came close to splashing over the sides with each movement.

"Around the corner the carriage raced," Gideon said, swinging both arms for emphasis. "The driver screamed for people to get out of the way." He stopped to take a drink and then continued. "I wasn't sure what to do, so I pulled my horse back and then, without thinking, I jumped onto the back of one of the stallions that pulled the carriage."

The more Gideon spoke, the stronger his brogue became. The Scot often exaggerated stories, but it made them more entertaining. Camren tried to imagine how someone seated on one horse, could catapult and jump on another, one that was racing by no less.

"What happened next?" he asked when Gideon hesitated to allow the question.

"I pulled and pulled on the reins, but the animal was mad with fear. The Devil must have been nearby, I swear it. So, I whistled as loud as I could, and they slowed and finally stopped."

"This happened at Hyde Park?" Camren looked at his friend. It was impossible to think there was enough distance at the heavily populated locale for a stampede.

"Aye, it was."

"What of your horse?"

"Can you believe it?" Gideon said. "The carriage driver did not offer me a ride back to my horse. Instead, the driver said I'd caused the ladies in the carriage to be overly distressed."

Shaking his head, Gideon lowered to a chair that automatically looked comically small under the large Scot. Camren eyed the spindly legs for a moment.

"The English are perpetually distressed."

"Indeed," Gideon exclaimed, holding up his glass.

"The horse?" Camren asked again.

Gideon's face fell. "I lost it. Have no idea where the animal went."

"You lost one of our horses then." Camren stood and went to the door. His valet looked up from where he sat by the door reading. "Daniel, can you go see about the black horse? It seems Mister Sutherland has... misplaced it at Hyde Park."

"The black horse returned earlier this afternoon, Sir," Daniel replied, and his eyes widened. "I apologize. We thought Mister Sutherland had released him upon arriving."

It was a fair assumption as Gideon had been in his cups days earlier and had tried to tether the horse to the front door. The animal had backed away and wandered about the gardens before being found.

"I see. Very well then." Camren went back into the parlor.

Gideon stood with arms stretched up. "Good thing for intelligent beasts. I will seek my bed. It has been a long day."

"Do you not wish the housekeeper to see about any injuries?" Camren asked, studying Gideon's clean and unwrinkled clothing.

"I don't wish to be a bother," Gideon said with a smile. He winked and left the room.

Camren was convinced Gideon had been in the pub chasing women and had somehow been the cause of the horses to spook.

Knowing his friend, he'd tried to stop the carriage while making matters worse. Camren shook his head and decided despite Gideon's penchant for strange adventures, he enjoyed having him there in London.

"A message for you," Daniel said, holding a tray with a crisp envelope upon it.

It was late in the evening and strange for a missive to be delivered so late. Camren opened the paper to find an invitation to The Lyon's Den, a gambling hall. His lips curved. "Thank you, Daniel. This is the perfect cure for boredom."

His valet's arched brow did little to dampen the good news that gave him a reason to venture out.

Having to come to London on an extended trip to see about his whisky business was tedious. He preferred the open land of his homeland in northern Scotland to the crowded city life of London.

He kept busy in Scotland, so he was rarely bored. There were many things that had to be tended to back at home and although his clan was at peace, there were the never-ending disputes between villagers and farmers.

Then there were the constant requests for arrangements between his family and other clans insisting on forming alliances by marriage.

As new laird of the clan, his first pronouncement had been to his two brothers and one sister. They would marry the match of their choice not one for gain to the clan.

It had been an easy decision, as he'd been in an arranged marriage that ended disastrously. His wife had run off with the man she'd been in love with and he'd been left humiliated in front of the entire clan.

After two years, the church had granted him a divorce, which freed him to marry again. He would do so because, more than anything, he wanted a family. The next time he married, it would be to a reliable, honest woman who loved him.

Glancing at the invitation, Camren scratched his chin. Why would this woman, the infamous Widow of Whitehall, invite him to gamble? Her establishment was well known for challenges and interesting high-stakes games. It was the perfect place for wealthy young men who needed a challenge or bored older men like him.

His lips curved at the quickening of his heart. Gideon must have crossed paths with someone who informed the Widow of their presence in London.

"Daniel, was there another invitation?"

His valet nodded. "One for Mister Sutherland."

"Of course."

"I suppose it will be an interesting thing to do tomorrow after-noon."

Daniel frowned. "I hear the games can be daunting, some even dangerous. You should reconsider going to that place, Laird."

"I understand the stakes can be daring, but I am astute enough to know which risks not to take. I will never risk anything that would affect my holdings in Scotland or more than I can afford to pay from my London account. Don't worry."

The valet looked to the side in thought. "I've heard the Widow has her ways of contriving the games, making them irresistible to the players."

"So I've heard." Camren took the last sip of whisky and studied the flames in the hearth. He could hardly wait to go and see what awaited him at The Lyon's Den.

Would he best the Widow or would he lose something precious?

CHAPTER THREE

MEOW. MEOW.

Like a timepiece, Lucille woke her up at exactly six in the morning. The cat rubbed its face against Evangeline's check, purring loudly. Despite the bit of annoyance, she had to smile at her feline's ability to maintain a strict schedule.

"I am getting up," she said and sat up. With eyes half-closed, she reached for her peach-colored robe and slid her feet into slippers. Lucille raced in front of Evangeline as she half-stumbled down the stairs and through the parlor and to the French doors. She pulled them open and the cat dashed out to the garden.

Leaving the doors cracked just wide enough for the cat to return inside, she went to the kitchen.

Martha looked up from the kitchen table and smiled. "Good morning. I will pour you a cup of tea."

"Don't fret, I can do it." Part of Evangeline's morning routine was to spend a few moments in quiet companionship, sipping tea until Lucille returned inside. Evangeline then fed her cat bits of meat left from the dinner the night before. Once that was done, she went back to her room to get dressed for the day.

"Mum and Father are plotting to marry me off," Evangeline said in a flat tone. "I doubt they will find someone willing."

Martha studied her for a long moment. "The only reason you remain single is because of your stubborn nature, Miss Genie. One small mistake does not a lonely life make."

The rather unfortunate incident had been more than a small mistake. She'd been without thought and much too adventurous for polite society.

"My small mistake, as you put it, was not in the least bit small." Evangeline giggled. "I was promiscuous and was found out in the worst way. Although there are many who practice sexual freedoms in what used to be my circle of friends, it was smartly kept behind closed doors."

They were quiet for a long moment. "And precisely why I think most men would find you irresistible. There won't be any boring moments with you."

"Martha!" Evangeline exclaimed, this time allowing laughter to escape. "If Mother heard you, she would swoon."

The older woman chuckled. "I am stating the truth. If gentlemen have not come with intentions, it is only because of the public nature of your escapade. Otherwise, they'd be flocking."

Lucille sauntered in and looked to Evangeline with expectation.

"After breakfast, I plan to question Mother. She will tell me exactly what she's plotting. I do not need to marry. I am perfectly happy to remain here enjoying a quiet life."

"Is that so?" Martha gave her a pointed look. "I would think you would welcome the company of a man."

Evangeline shook her head. "Of my choosing, yes. But not one like that horrible Mortimer Witt."

Martha nodded. "I must speak freely to agree the man was most disagreeable. However, most men are not, and I will pray that you are matched with one who is caring and a good person."

"Thank you," Evangeline said with a grimace. "You can also pray that I be left to do as I wish and not marry at all."

While heading down the hall and up the stairs, Evangeline kept considering what it would be like to actually marry and have to live somewhere else. She adored her home and the thought of a home elsewhere was unthinkable. Up until the day before, she'd thought her parents were fine with her remaining with them. They'd never be alone when growing old as she would be there to look after them.

Fran had laid out a violet morning gown and a delicate, sheer white shawl. The freckle-faced maid stood next to the dresser with brush in one hand and a ribbon in the other. "I will braid your hair up and use this ribbon through it. It will be so very pretty."

"Thank you," Evangeline said, not caring one way or the other as she did not expect to see anyone outside the home. If she were to be honest, spending the day in her sleeping gown would have been preferable.

After dressing, she sat dutifully, allowing the maid to braid her hair and give her the news of the day. Early every morning, Fran and Martha went to the market where they caught up with all the goings-on from other maids. Evangeline felt bad for her staff as they rarely had anything exciting to report.

"There are two new gentlemen in town that are all the talk of the town," Fran said with an exaggerated sigh. "They are Scottish and reputed to be roguish."

Scots were normally not the talk of society. Unless they were titled, they were still considered quite uncivilized. "Why are they so popular? Let me guess, they are both handsome."

"Yes, exactly," Fran replied. "Extremely, especially the laird, his name is Camren Mac... something. I do not recall."

"I see. And they are wealthy?"

Fran sighed. "Oh, yes. Breathtakingly handsome and with plenty of coin. They are often spotted about town, riding massive horses that are not quite the perfect beasts for city life."

Fran gave up the pretense of continuing to do Evangeline's hair and sat on a chair leaning forward, her features bright. "The other Scot, his name is Gideon Sutherland, came upon a carriage with his unruly beast late yesterday. It spooked the carriage horses so badly that they bolted. Lady Beatrice and her daughter, Lenora, were frightened horribly by the incident."

Evangeline pressed her lips together, not wishing to smile at the picture conjured in her mind. Lady Beatrice was old society and had no doubt spoke to the authorities. The constable was probably knocking on the Scotsmen's door this morning.

"I wonder why they are here. It's likely they have more to do than to annoy Londoners."

Fran's eyes widened with excitement. "Molly, the Robertsons' maid, told me she heard they are here on business. Scottish whisky. They are also gamblers, going to that horrible place on Whitehall Street."

At the mention of the place, Evangeline frowned. "The most curious of people go there. I've always wished to meet Missus Dove-Lyon. I bet she has the best stories and insight into London society."

"You could never," Fran exclaimed, her eyes rounded. "The very thought of it. Your parents would never allow you to leave the house again."

Losing her only regular outing to the bookstore would be unbearable. "True, I have little to look forward to as it is."

Her parents were already at the breakfast table when Evangeline entered the dining room. Both smiled at her warmly which was normal, but there was an underlying current in the air.

She served herself from the sideboard as was their custom and sat. A shy young maid poured juice for her.

"You look lovely in lilac," her mother said. "I will ensure to have another gown made for you in that shade."

Her father looked up from the papers he was reading. "Indeed. I agree."

"I wish to speak to both of you about this marriage nonsense." Evangeline took a sip of her juice, allowing for her parents to exchange a look. Unfortunately, she could not tell what, exactly, was communicated between them.

She continued. "I do not wish to marry at all, but to remain here in this home. When you both are elderly, I will be here to care for you."

"We have quite a few years before we require care," her father replied with earnest. "Your mother has even longer before she needs to worry. I look forward knowing she will care for me as she is still young and beautiful."

Olivia Prescott blushed prettily and smiled at her husband. "I agree. Don't fret about caring for us dear. You deserve to be in love and to form a family of your own."

"Men prefer to marry women they are proud to be seen with in public. I will not mince words, as we have always been honest with each other. I love you both very much and am eternally grateful for your having forgiven my missteps of the past. However, society is not as forgiving, and no one will marry me unless forced."

"Nonsense. You are a lovely girl…" her father started.

"There is a way for someone to marry you and it will be his choice." Her mother interrupted, pinning Evangeline with a pointed look. "Your father and I have made up our minds and will not bend on this. You are to be married because we wish you to be happy."

Her stomach sank, the food on her plate unappetizing. She pushed it away and let out a long breath. "You cannot force happiness, Mother."

"We will see." Her mother's cryptic reply made Evangeline nervous.

"What are you planning?"

Her father gave her an indulgent look. "Isn't today your book club meeting, Genie? Eat up. I will drive you there when I leave in about an hour."

The subject was closed.

Evangeline drank the rest of her juice and when her stomach grumbled, she picked up the toast and nibbled on it. She'd confront her mother later. First, she'd discuss it with Rose and come up with the best way to combat the issue intelligently.

Her friend was a perfect negotiator and would give her good rebuttals and excuses for not marrying.

"I AGREE WITH your parents," Rose pronounced with a firm nod later that morning. "We should all seek to be married and not be alone in life. Especially you."

They were seated at a small table in the back of the bookstore. The others had not arrived yet, so it was nice and quiet. Jarod, the shopkeeper, had let them in and after greeting them, had returned to the front of the shop.

Evangeline's bottom jaw dropped. "You can't be..."

"You, my friend, are a passionate woman who requires the presence of a strong, virile man in your life."

It was certainly not at all what Evangeline expected. She narrowed her eyes at her friend. "You knew. Mother spoke to you, didn't she? You were the errand she ran yesterday and insisted on going alone."

Rose shook her head. "I did not see your mother yesterday. The only time we have spoken about marriage has been in your presence. If you recall, I've always maintained that you and I should marry." At saying this, Rose glanced toward the front of the shop.

"In that case, I believe you should have a chat with a certain someone." Evangeline motioned toward Jarod.

Her friend gave her a droll look and flipped the page in the book she held. "Where are the others? They should be here by now."

It was almost eleven. They always met at ten in the morning. Evangeline scanned the small shop. They were the only ones in there besides Jarod. Just a few moments later, the bell over the door jingled and an older man walked in. As he browsed, the other two members of the book club arrived. Sisters Harriett and Ramona entered and greeted Jarod before quickly making their way to the back of the store where Evangeline and Rose sat.

"You will never guess what happened," Harriett, the eldest of the sisters, exclaimed.

"One of the Scottish gentlemen stopped us to ask for directions," Ramona said, her faced flushed. "He spoke directly to me."

Evangeline narrowed her eyes. "Why would that be something of note? People ask for directions all the time."

The sisters exchanged looks and Harriett spoke. "If you saw them, you'd understand. They are overwhelming. In stance and features."

"I see." Evangeline slid a look to Rose, who, like her, seemed to find the sisters' story incredible.

Rose let out a breath. "Pray tell, where were they wishing to go?"

"A tailor," the sisters replied at the same time.

"We gave them directions to Middleton's."

After a continued conversation about the Scottish men, Evangeline gathered both were tall, wide-shouldered men. One had red hair, the other light brown. Although reputed to be rogues, neither had been seen with a woman, nor had they visited any questionable locales since their arrival.

"The laird is named Camren Maclean. He had hazel eyes and a deep voice. The other, Gideon Sutherland, was the friendlier and more approachable of the two." The sisters took turns informing them while finishing each other's sentences.

With all the information the sisters insisted on dispensing, Evangeline had no need to meet either of them as she was sure to know them already.

By the end of their book club meeting, they'd discussed very little about the book, which was fine with Evangeline as she enjoyed the company of her friends and it mattered little to her what they discussed.

They walked out and bid farewell to Ramona and Harriett, who hurried off in search of a pastry shop.

"Should we go for a walk around the park before returning?" Rose asked. "Or perhaps hire an open carriage. It is a such beautiful day and I detest the idea of returning home just yet."

Preferring to ride so that people would not stare, Evangeline agreed to hiring a carriage.

THE DRIVER TOOK them around the park at a slow, casual pace, giving them time to look around and greet anyone they knew. For the most part, most of the people at the park were on horseback or on foot.

Couples sat on benches with chaperones nearby, stealing a touch of a hand or a delicate nudge of the shoulder. A lady with two daughters strolled leisurely as the mother kept a keen eye out for any single gentlemen that might happen by.

Evangeline let out a sigh. There had been a time she'd enjoyed walking there. She'd not been as innocent as the couple on the bench. Instead, she'd found the park a perfect place to meet with Lord Avery Hamilton, a man who willingly played along with her foolish games of seduction.

Her reputation had not been in tatters then, as they had been very careful. Lord Hamilton and she were madly in love, or so she'd thought. They'd not become betrothed because he was expected to marry someone of his elevated status. Although he did promise they would run away together and marry, it had not come to pass as yet.

When she and Rose rode past a specific area of the park, Rose slide a side-glance in Evangeline's direction. "There have been other scandals. Some much worse than yours."

"I am sure. However, once a woman's reputation is in tatters, there is little to do to repair it. Other than leave London I suppose."

"What, exactly, happened that day? You've only told me bits and pieces."

Evangeline let out a long breath and began talking in a low voice.

It had started as her encounters normally did. She'd meet Avery Hamilton at Hyde Park and then join him in his personal carriage. His driver took them from there to a secluded destination Avery claimed to have scouted out to ensure plenty of privacy. It was part of the thrill, to have encounters in places one would normally not.

This time, they had agreed to an encounter outdoors. First, they would undress in the carriage, dash out and enjoy nature, as one could put it, and finally, they'd hurry back to the carriage.

It had gone terribly wrong.

Too busy enjoying the moment on a blanket just below a small ridge, they'd not heard a group of young ladies approach above them.

The birdwatchers and their tutors had come up to the edge of the ridge and gotten a clear view of Evangeline and her partner. Although the tutors did their best to keep impressionable girls from seeing such a scene, the girls had not listened and were eager to see what happened.

Hearing a gasp, Evangeline had looked up to see ten sets of eyes staring down at them.

Like a horrible dream, she'd fought to stop Avery who thought it was part of the game and not listened. Not at first. When she'd tried to scramble away, he'd pulled her back by the leg, laughing and climbing atop her.

"People are watching," she'd finally said, the words hard to get out past the lack of air in her lungs.

Things got progressively worse at that point. Avery had jumped up and stood bare as day. The girls began shrieking.

One of the tutors had stepped too close to the edge and in her to attempt to calm her charges, lost her balance and fell over the incline. The rather large woman had landed right on top of Evangeline, crushing her right leg.

"What happened then?" Rose asked.

"Avery Hamilton rushed to the carriage and rode off. I remained behind, not able to move, and without clothing." Evangeline shook her head. "I will never forget that day. The poor woman struggling to breathe while trying to roll me up in the blanket."

Prudence giggled. "Up until the group showed up, I bet it was fun."

She couldn't help but smile. "It was. However, ill advised."

"I remember those days. We were all young and foolish," Rose said with a sigh. "I was never brave enough to go that far, however."

The clip-clopping of the horse's hooves, the warm air and sunny, clear sky reminded Evangeline of days past and she had to admit longing for adventure.

"I often wonder why your mother allows you to continue your friendship with me," Evangeline said. She'd repeated that line over the years. No matter what happened, Rose had never stopped visiting or spending time in public with her. It had been during her recovery that they'd become closer than ever.

Her friend's blue eyes sparkled. "Because she loves you and your mother. Besides, she told me to envy your vigor for life."

Evangeline smiled. "No, she did not!"

Rose giggled. "All right, I made that up."

"Had I known one of the encounters would have left my reputation ruined and my leg deformed, I would have reconsidered." She shrugged. "The worst is how it hurt my parents."

"It's all in the past," Rose soothed. "Now your mother feels sure she can find you a husband."

"That, I do find hard to believe. I am sure whoever the poor man is, once he finds out who I am, he will fight to escape."

Both laughed. Evangeline gave the driver directions to take them home as she had to find time to speak to her mother and put her off the idea of marriage.

In that moment, the largest horses Evangeline had ever seen blocked their path.

The beasts were impressive and, immediately, she knew who was astride them.

When her gaze clashed with a hazel one, she became acutely aware the sisters had not been exaggerating in the least.

Camren Maclean was indeed breathtakingly handsome.

With a blank expression, his gaze traveled across from her to Rose. He gave a curt nod and motioned to the carriage driver to continue forth.

Evangeline locked gazes with him for but a moment and then studied his companion, who was also attractive in a more rugged manner. This one smiled at them and winked at Rose.

"Oh, my," Rose said. "The man is very forward."

Evangeline made sure to keep her gaze straight ahead, but her lips curved. "He winked at you. How refreshing."

"Oh, hush," Rose exclaimed, covering her mouth to hide her grin.

CHAPTER FOUR

Upon entering The Lyon's Den, Camren and Gideon were greeted by two young, attractive women dressed in revealing low cut gowns.

"Welcome, gentlemen," a blonde woman greeted them with a well-practiced batting of her lashes. "I am Isadora." She motioned to a redhead who, like her, acted as if she were engrossed by their appearance.

"This is Monica. We will escort you to meet Mrs. Dove-Lyon. If there is anything you require, we are here to serve your every need."

Camren and Gideon exchanged a knowing look and followed the swaying hips into a parlor of sorts.

"Mrs. Dove-Lyon will be with you momentarily," a servant announced and walked out silently; his footsteps absorbed by the thick carpeting.

Their escorts lounged on chaises ensuring perfect poses while Camren and Gideon remained standing.

Both bowed at the waist upon an elegant woman entering. Mrs. Dove-Lyon's keen eyes rested on Gideon for a long moment before focusing on Camren.

"Please sit," she said, taking a chair next to the fireplace. "Thank you for accepting my invitation. As you may have gathered, this is an unusual establishment. It may or may not be to your liking. That, I will leave for you to decide." She hesitated as the blonde woman stood and served them drinks. Once she returned to her chaise, the redhead rose and took a tray from a servant. She then placed it down on the table between Camren and Gideon. The aroma of tiny meat pies filled the air.

Camren was impressed that upon tasting the whisky, he recognized it as his own.

The woman smiled. "I only serve the best, and your whisky is without compare. I plan to stock it at my establishment. My business associate will be in touch about that."

"Thank you," Camren replied.

Gideon cleared his throat. "Are the rumors true, that the stakes at your tables are high, sometimes even dangerous?"

"I cater to a very special clientele. I admit to satisfying the needs of the wealthy and bored. However, most of my guests are gentlemen like yourselves who are adventurous."

Despite himself, Camren's interest was piqued.

Moments later, they were seated at a round table, cards in hand. Admittedly, both were cautious in placing their bets, not sure of the room and other players.

There was an interesting combination of men in the room, from older to extremely young. All had the same thing in common, extraordinary wealth.

At one table, a man stood with a glass in his hand. The entire room went silent and watched.

The goblet was filled with a thick, red liquid.

"Is that blood?" Gideon whispered to Camren.

"I believe so."

The man held the cup up and glared at another across the table.

His face went pale as he brought the item to his lips.

Everyone watched as he drank the liquid, stopping on occasion to gag. Somehow, he managed to keep it down.

"You are not permitted to leave the room," a man who now held the empty goblet on a tray told him. "Else you will have to repeat."

The unfortunate man turned green and gagged several times, struggling not to lose the contents of his stomach. "May I have some water?"

Someone pushed a glass of water into his hand and he downed the contents and slowly lowered into his chair.

Everyone returned to their games, including the man who'd drank the blood.

"Interesting," Camren said as a new set of men sat at his table to start a new game.

Gideon frowned at the newcomers. "What is at stake for this game?"

"Marriage," the young man who'd introduced himself as Lord Lloyd Whitaker replied. "We were specifically chosen because we are single and without attachments."

Camren and Gideon exchanged looks.

Gideon turned an interesting shade of red. "I am not about to marry someone because of a game."

There were four other men besides him at the table and Camren felt a rush of adrenaline. It had been a long time since any kind of excitement rushed through his veins. "I'm in."

"Are you mad?" Gideon placed a hand on his shoulder. "Don't forget, you are a laird." Then he added, "With responsibilities to our clan."

"That makes this game even more interesting." The youngest man at the table leaned forward with an expectant expression. "You, Sir, may have more to lose than the rest of us."

"My freedom is precious to me," another said. "I am not sure I can risk it."

Mrs. Dove-Lyon approached with a smile stretched across her face. "I come to sweeten the pot, per se," she said, waving a hand. Dangling from her fingers on a velvet ribbon was a key. "Whoever wins this game will get a beautiful townhouse in the most prominent of districts, St. James' Square." There was a collective intake of breath, except for Camren and Gideon who had no desire to own more property in England.

The woman dangled the key for a moment longer. Her keen gaze moved to each man at the table. "The loser must marry a beautiful woman within a week."

The men eyed each other. It was probable that most of them could afford a townhouse, but the address the woman spouted out was, indeed, one of the most desirable of addresses.

Camren wasn't interested in owning the house. He would probably sell it upon winning. He eyed his competition. The men maintained a calm demeaner, but he spotted a faint line of sweat beads on the lip of one. Another swallowed hard, his nostrils spreading with nerves. From the easy to read signs, he could win the game easily.

"What is the opening bid?" The lord, who Camren considered would be a valid opponent, asked.

"Your home. Place the key to your current property on the table," Mrs. Dove-Lyon said.

"So, the loser not only loses their home, but has to marry?"

"No," Mrs. Dove-Lyon replied with a smile. "You see, the last two will bid their homes in hopes to win this house." She swung the key. "The loser will get a wife and I will allow him to retain his home. I must remind you, she is the loveliest of creatures."

His heart thundered and Camren was amazed that he considered entering the game. It was the most interesting and unexpected turn of events. Even Gideon seemed intrigued. He leaned forward, staring at the key intently.

Four keys were placed in the center of the table. Gideon, who didn't have a townhome in London, was asked to wager the cost of a home. He did so without complaint.

"One deal, one replacement each round, no more than two cards." Mrs. Dove-Lyon motioned to a man who dealt cards to each of them.

The men studied their cards, each without expression, their eyes moving to the others in search of a clue to what they held. Several, including Camren, requested replacements of one or two cards.

Camren began to wonder whether to bluff or keep his hand. It wasn't a grand one, but good enough to win if he played right.

Two men dropped out immediately and were obviously annoyed at how quickly they'd lost their homes. Camren figured they'd be entering another game in hopes of winning them back.

Of the remaining three, they were once again allowed to replace a card. Lord Whitaker was the only one who did so and then threw his cards down with a look of disgust.

However, he recovered quickly, watching as both Gideon and Camren exchanged incredulous looks.

"This is not going to turn out well," Gideon grumbled.

"Do not think of me as your laird, but as your opponent right now," Camren said, hoping to throw his friend off balance.

Everyone in the room turned to watch as Mrs. Dove-Lyon offered them the opportunity once again to exchange a card. "This is your last chance," she exclaimed theatrically.

What was he doing? If he lost the game, he'd have to marry. As laird, the woman would have to move to Scotland, away from London. Had her father lost a wager and put his daughter up as payment? He had so many questions.

Forcing himself to focus, he placed one card on the table. Not sure why, other than it would not hurt if he got a worse card. At least, he hoped it wouldn't.

Gideon did the same. They were too much alike.

When he lifted the card, his spirits soared. He'd witness his roguish friend being married. His lips almost curved, but he managed to keep from it.

"Show your hand." The woman motioned to him.

Camren placed his cards on the table face up. A feeling of satisfaction came over him while at the same time feeling a bit badly for his friend.

When Gideon's eyes widened, Camren wasn't sure what to think. The expression of shock was hard to read.

"Now show yours," the woman said.

Ever so slowly, Gideon lowered his cards.

This time, it was Camren who paled.

"Sorry, Laird," Gideon said. "But I am thankful not to have to get married."

Camren had lost the game.

There was a collective intake of breath around the room, several clearings of throats as it seemed most felt badly for him.

How had it been that plans for an afternoon of gaming had garnered him the loss of the very first game he'd entered. Additionally, not only did he lose to his best friend, but the idiot was now grinning like a loon.

"Whisky," he said hoarsely, and a glass was pushed into his hand. He swallowed it and held it out to be refilled.

The young opponent at the table gave him a pitying look. "You have a week to marry her or to figure out a way out of it."

"There is no way out of it," Mrs. Dove-Lyon emphasized. "It is a house rule that you cannot bet away a prize gotten from a loss."

"A woman is not a prize to be lost or won. We are speaking of a human being." Camren couldn't believe they were playing for things like marriage.

Mrs. Dove-Lyon didn't seem affected by his statement. "You are correct and that is why we only gamble marriage at the woman's request."

He looked to Gideon whose eyebrows disappeared into his hair-line.

"Have these women asked to be prizes in these games? I don't understand."

Mrs. Dove-Lyon had moved away, seeming bored with the conversation. So, an older gentleman answered his question. "The women who come to Mrs. Dove-Lyon in search of a husband are those with less than stellar reputations. A scandal or past misstep can ruin a woman's chances for marriage in London society."

"That is such English absurdity," Gideon replied. "We allow our women more freedoms."

The man shrugged. "It is not fair, I agree."

Camren lost any interest to continue playing and went to the side of the room where a bar was set up. The man behind it poured him whisky without asking. He mulled over what to do while watching the games continuing. At one table, the men had placed daggers in the center. He wondered what losing at that table meant. At another, each man had a shot glass of green liquid in front of him.

This was certainly the most unique of establishments.

The man behind the bar placed a second drink in front of him. "You will call on her tomorrow. All the pertinent information will be delivered to your home tonight."

"And what if I don't do it," Camren said to the man who looked past him to where Mrs. Dove-Lyon stood.

"You will, you are a laird and man of your word."

He couldn't argue with that. He would do it, would marry and return to Scotland at the end of the season with an English wife.

The consequences would be nominal if he were to be honest. His clan was not at war, nor did they harbor any resentments toward the English. Being connected to one of the larger and powerful Maclean Clans meant protection and being left alone by any would-be attackers.

It was only by guarding the most northern border that his warriors found a reprieve from boredom. Other than that, training for competition in the games gave them have a reason to remain in shape.

Gideon finished playing at the table with the green liquid and came to stand next to him. "That was vile. The excretion of some plant that is supposed to make one faint."

"You didn't drink?"

"Aye, I did. Still waiting." Gideon remained upright and not seeming to feel badly. A thud sounded, followed by a second as two men from that table collapsed. The third succumbed, leaving only the winner and Gideon standing.

"Do you want to sit?" Camren asked.

"Nay," Gideon said and motioned to the bar. "Whisky."

They left an hour later. The men who'd drunk the green liquid had all been roused and carried out. Gideon swayed a bit, but Camren considered that he'd drank quite a bit of whisky, and that could be the cause not the green drink.

After mounting, they headed in search of the townhouse Gideon had won. The Scot would be the target of many a mother searching for a rich husband. With an impressive address and a bank account to match, Gideon would soon be on London society's map as the most eligible bachelor.

If not for his current predicament, Camren would be gleeful about Gideon's new status. Nonetheless, there would be a bit of satisfaction in knowing he wasn't the only one about to fall into a trap set by London society.

He'd inform his friend later that evening.

CHAPTER FIVE

"MOTHER, YOU CAN'T be seriously allowing me to marry a man neither of us have met." Evangeline could barely believe the explanation her mother had just given her. She'd gone to a matchmaker. Mrs. Dove-Lyon, a woman who had a reputation for running a business that everyone whispered about.

Her mother's soft smile made Evangeline wonder if her mother had been drinking too much sherry that morning.

"Wear the new lilac gown. It was delivered yesterday. The color is perfect for you. Your soon to be husband will arrive later this afternoon."

"I will certainly not." Evangeline stomped over to her mother. "Has everyone lost their minds? Why would you and Father ever agree to something like this?"

Her mother's direct gaze was clear. "Because unless we get you married, you will find a lover and what will happen then? Living openly in sin? It would be disastrous for our family."

"A… lover?" Evangeline let out a breath in an effort to rein in her temper. "I am not a harlot to be kept away from men. I go out every single week to my book club and to the market with Martha or Fran.

Since that horrible day, I have been nothing short of a nun."

When her mother chuckled, Evangeline had to press her lips together and bite back a cuss word. "Darling girl, that is why you need to be married. You are not the type to spend your days locked in this house or in a dusty bookshop. Just try to be cordial for me. Let us see what happens today."

Her mother was right. Every night, she dreamed of being carried away by a handsome stranger, being made love to until both were rendered breathless. Sometimes, she'd waken overheated and had to stand by the open window allowing the fresh breeze to fan over her nude body.

The things she'd fantasized about had sent her reeling with want on some occasions.

"Who is he?" she blurted.

Her mother's smile widened. "You will be pleased. However, I will not disclose his identity to you. I think it's best you find out upon his arrival."

"Seriously, Mother, why all the mystery?"

Without replying and having an impish grin on her face, her mother swept from the room, motioning for Fran to enter. "Help her into the lilac dress. Ensure her hair is swept up, allowing a few curls to fall onto her shoulders."

"My mother the fashion expert," Evangeline grumbled.

"Isn't this exciting," Fran exclaimed, hurrying over to help her out of her morning gown. "I wonder who your suitor is."

Evangeline frowned at her reflection in the mirror. "Probably a toad who no one will marry unless they are forced to."

"Oh, no," Fran said with conviction. "He will be handsome and will sweep you off your feet the instant you meet."

The lilac gown fit her body perfectly. The bodice emphasized her plump breasts and closed in on her waist. The skirting fell effortlessly over her hips. Evangeline couldn't believe how the dress transformed her body to look normal, unhindered.

"Your mother knows how to pick a gown for you, doesn't she?" Fran teased.

"Until I walk, I will admit it does make me look normal."

Humming the entire time, Fran pulled Evangeline's golden hair up into a simple but flattering style, allowing several strands to fall naturally to her shoulders as her mother had instructed.

CAMREN ARRIVED AT 29 Hart Street at precisely two in the afternoon as per his instructions. He was greeted at the door by a footman. Just inside the door stood an elegant blonde woman, the barely noticeable gray strands in her upswept blonde hair and soft laugh lines did little to distract from her beauty.

"Welcome, Laird. I am Olivia Prescott." She smiled at him and he bowed slightly to her. "Please come in. My daughter is in the drawing room." He was just about to ask if she was the one he was to marry. He would not have minded getting to know the woman, although she was definitely older than him.

She paused just a few steps further. "My daughter is not aware of your identity, but I did tell her you are the man she is to marry. I am hopeful that after spending time alone, you and she will find each other suitable."

"You are aware that I lost a game and that is how I come to be here?" Camren asked.

The woman nodded. "Yes, fully. Each man at the table was hand-picked by me."

Understanding dawned and he prepared himself for the woman in the drawing room, just on the other side of the slightly open doors.

Whomever the woman was, was probably lacking in every way.

"May I have a moment?"

"Of course," the woman replied, not seeming at all taken aback by his request. "Why don't you go into my husband's study and then enter through double doors that connect into the sitting room when you are ready?"

She motioned to a doorway and then walked away.

Camren paced the length of the small room, wishing to be any-where but there. If only there was a way out of the predicament he'd gotten himself into. He was not a coward nor would he ever go back on his word. However, this was a situation that he'd never thought to be caught in.

He blew out a long breath and reached for the doorknob.

Upon opening it and stepping into the sunlit room, he did not see anyone right away. His first thought was that the woman had gotten upset at his hesitance and left.

Then movement by a set of French doors caught his attention. Just outside stood a vision in lilac. The young woman was bent at the waist petting a huge, orange cat.

"Lucille, how did you get out? What a sly little devil you are."

Camren studied the younger version Olivia Prescott. She was womanly, her breasts full and her waist slender. She was not a waif, which pleased him.

Seeming to sense his perusal, she straightened and stared at him with wide, green eyes.

"Miss Prescott, I am Laird Camren Maclean," he said, bending at the waist.

Her lips parted and she leaned to the side to look past him. When not seeing anyone, she met his gaze and then looked away. Her chest lifted and lowered and when she took a step and swayed, he reached out.

"I'm fine. I am not about to swoon."

Then taking several more steps with a pronounced limp, she entered the room.

Only English society would find a limp to be a reason for someone as beautiful as her not to be marriageable.

"Would you like something to drink?" She went to a sideboard. "I need something…"

She poured sherry into two glasses and held one out for him.

Camren accepted it, noting she'd yet to give him her full name. "What is your first name?"

"They didn't give you any information either?" She looked surprised.

"No, only the address and time to be here."

She drank the sherry down in two sips and motioned to a chair. "Would you please sit? Your height makes my neck hurt."

The young woman was outspoken. He liked that she did not hesitate to speak her mind. "After you."

They sat in chairs facing one another.

"My name is Evangeline." She didn't elaborate as to whether there was a second name.

"Your name suits you perfectly," he replied, meeting her gaze. "It's beautiful."

She let out a breath. "Thank you."

"Did you ask your mother to do this?" He tried to keep his voice even, not sure why he found fault in the idea of a woman forcing a man into marriage.

She lifted her pert nose into the air. "No, Sir, I did not. Nor do I agree with this entire charade. I must ask, why would you?"

Once again, Camren was intrigued by her reply. If she'd not put her mother up for it, then she was probably not willing to go through with it. That could mean a good ending to all of it. However, for some reason, he couldn't stop wondering what it would be like to have her in his bed.

"It was not my best decision, I will admit."

"Hmph. I often wonder why men are supposed to be the superior sex." She shrugged. "My mother met with the priest this morning. We are to marry in six days. Other than lightning befalling one of us, we will have to go through with it."

She didn't seem overly unhappy with the situation. He'd describe it as put-off or annoyed by it.

"You seem to have accepted it then?" he asked, studying where her fingers touched when she rubbed the base of her throat. His gaze lingered there for a moment and then trailed to the top of her creamy breasts. Not wishing to be caught, he quickly looked away.

"Accepted it? No, but I am a realist. There is little way to stop it. However, I am sure we are intelligent enough to perhaps figure a way out of this… situation."

Her gaze moved from his face down his chest and followed the length of his outstretched leg. It was the most sensual thing he'd experienced in a very long time.

"Tell me, Miss Prescott, why was there a need for your parents to go to such great lengths to marry you off?"

She shrugged. "They seem to think I should not enjoy living here and remaining single. Which is what I've accepted. If no one offered for my hand when I was younger, it will not happen now."

He continued. "Is English society so shallow to allow your limp to overshadow your beauty?"

Just then, the orange cat sauntered through the open doors and into the room. Its green eyes looked him over. Seeming to find him lacking, the cat then turned away and walked out the door into the main house.

"There are stronger reasons for my being single, Laird. I am not prepared to speak of them. I will tell you that my limp is involved. I am sure if pressed, anyone in our social circles will happily fill you in on the details of my fall from grace."

"I would prefer to hear it from you."

Her lips curved and he could not look away. The woman was exquisite. "Then you will have to wait."

"Tell me about your cat."

She looked toward the doorway, where the animal just walked through. "How about we sit in the garden? I will ring for something light. I have not eaten since morning."

Camren refrained from offering assistance to help her stand and she didn't seem to find affront. He motioned for her to walk ahead and, for a beat, she seemed unsure. However, when she stepped forward, he noticed it was her right leg that was affected. From just the little bit she'd said, her injury was linked with whatever had happened that brought ruin to her reputation.

Interesting.

EVANGELINE COULDN'T BELIEVE what was happening was real. The man exuded confidence. The rapid beating of her heart made her aware of the instant attraction to him.

That, in her opinion, meant she had to extricate herself from the situation as soon as possible. There wasn't any possibility that someone as able and virile as Camren Maclean would ever accept being trapped into marriage. The man was a laird, no less. In all probability, he had at least a dozen women back in Scotland with hopes of marriage.

If times were different and she was as daring as she was in the past, she would consider a tryst prior to calling off the wedding. But the twinge in her leg was a reminder of how different things were now.

Men were visual creatures, not attracted to women with physical shortcomings. She exaggerated her limp, swaying side to side unevenly, and actually found herself hunching her shoulders just enough to make it look as if she had trouble moving forward.

"Evangeline, stop it at once." Her mother was sitting under a shade tree and had caught sight of them. "Stand up straight and stop overstressing your limp."

She didn't look over her shoulder but thought she heard Camren chuckle. "My leg hurts," she replied, her face heating.

"I doubt it hurts that much," her mother replied.

"Would you like to join us for a light repast, Mother?" Evangeline gave up the pretense and continued toward a table under a shade tree.

"No, thank you. I am about to speak to Martha about dinner." She waltzed out of the garden with a soft smile toward the laird. "My daughter is quite clever. Do not be put off by it."

"I find it refreshing," Camren replied.

They sat at a table under the shelter of a tree's shade. The weather was perfect, just warm enough she didn't need a heavy shawl, with a refreshing breeze.

As put off as she was by the situation, Evangeline had to admit Camren Maclean was exactly the type of man she would not mind sharing her bed with. She wasn't sure of forever, but he had promise of being a good lover.

Best to put those thoughts away. Although he didn't act bothered by her physical shortcomings, surely, he was just being polite.

"Why are you in London, Mr. Maclean? I assume you have a home in Scotland."

He nodded. His playful expression revealed he knew she wished to keep the conversation light. "I do have a large home in the Highlands, two attached villages and many acres of farms."

"I see, and the reason for coming to London?"

"I have a whisky distribution center here. I came on business and to spend a season here."

Mulling over what to say next, she decided it was best to change the subject. She didn't want to speak of the way he'd come across Mrs. Dove-Lyon and how he'd been trapped into marriage. It boggled her mind how a matchmaker could force a man's hand.

"Do you have brothers or sisters?"

He nodded. "Two brothers and one sister. My brothers are younger and live with me. My sister is older and married. She lives in a house within walking distance." He met her gaze. "I should ask the same in turn."

"You do not have to. I have one sister. She lives at one of our country estates. Have you met my father?"

He shook his head. "No. I am to meet him today at dinner."

Dinner. She'd not been warned that he'd remain for so long. Evangeline looked toward the doorway and wondered how rude it would be to go in search of her mother.

"My father and mother have both taken leave of their senses by signing me up to be married through a matchmaker. Do you not find it appalling?"

"In the Highlands, marriages are usually brokered by the lairds or patriarchs. Neither the groom nor the bride is involved, nor asked for their opinions. This is much like that."

"Why are you not betrothed then?"

His lips curved and the deep dimples that appeared on both cheeks took her aback. Evangeline had to tear her eyes away and she pretended a sudden interest in the foliage.

"I was married and then not. I am not betrothed now because my father died unexpectedly and had not made any provisions for a marriage agreement. It is expected that I will eventually marry a Sutherland. Our clans are allies, but we have not been joined by a marriage. Although it would strengthen our clans and double our warrior numbers, there is, in actuality, little to gain by a marriage alliance."

When she looked back to him, their eyes met for a moment too long.

"Here you are, some cheese and fruit. Dinner will be served in just a couple of hours." Fran gave a short curtsy, her face a crimson red when she slid a glance to Camren.

They were silent for a moment as Fran walked away. The girl moved at a snail's pace, no doubt hoping to hear something to share at the market the next day.

"Once we marry, I insist you return to Scotland with me." His tone left no room for misinterpretation. The laird had spoken, and she was expected to obey.

Evangeline's right brow rose, and she let out a breath.

"Is that so?"

CHAPTER SIX

"HOW WAS YOUR encounter?" Gideon did not bother hiding his curiosity. He'd rushed into the room as soon as Camren had returned home.

"Interesting." Camren accepted a drink from his friend. "I am not quite sure what to make of it."

The four hours he'd spent at the Prescott home had been rather pleasant. He'd enjoyed verbally sparring with Evangeline as she'd did her best to put him off without being overly disparaging.

Her father, an actuary, was quite knowledgeable in the matter of London finances and had given him plenty of solid advice regarding Camren's enterprises there. As a matter of fact, upon recognizing it was time to depart, he'd been reluctant to do so and had accepted the suggestion to play a game of faro with the family. The family banter reminded him of his own, which meant he thoroughly enjoyed himself.

"Are you daydreaming?" Gideon studied him with a perplexed expression, his eyes narrowed and his brows lowered. "What happened to you?"

Camren shook his head. "I actually enjoyed myself tremendously.

Miss Evangeline Prescott is as beautiful as Mrs. Dove-Lyon promised and not at all happy about the proposition of being married off."

There was a discreet knock and Daniel entered with a tray. "This note was just delivered."

Gideon reached for it and tore it open. "Another invitation. This time, it's to pay a call to the Monroe estate."

"Do we know them?" Camren asked Daniel who bit his bottom lip in thought.

"I do believe Lord Monroe is on the list of men you wished to speak to regarding the business. He is quite wealthy." Daniel shrugged. "A meeting was requested."

"Ah, yes, you are correct," Camren replied, going to his desk and sitting. He then shuffled papers until finding his diary. "We will accept the invitation."

THE MEN ARRIVED at the Monroe estate, having opted for a carriage instead of horseback. Ostentatious, ornate gates were opened, and the driver pulled through and directly to the front of an equally grandiose mansion. Huge marble lions on pillars presided over both sides of wide steps to an ornate front doorway.

Two footmen came to the carriage. One opened the door after the other placed a stepstool for them to use.

Both Camren and Gideon avoided the stool and stepped onto the graveled ground.

"Welcome to the Monroe estate," the footman said, bending at the waist until his face was level with the soil. The other one with stool in hand rushed to the front doors.

Gideon gave Camren a knowing look. It was going to be a trying visit, where they'd both have to be on their best behavior.

They were greeted in the foyer by another servant, this one obviously the butler. The man bowed, albeit not as low as the footman. Once they placed their calling cards on a tray, the butler asked that they follow him.

Once arriving at an archway, he loudly announced their names. "Laird Camren Maclean and Mister Gideon Sutherland."

Inside stood a pale man, his arm artfully placed over the back of a chair in which a brunette older woman sat. On a nearby chair was a younger woman who looked both him and Gideon over with unhidden curiosity.

Camren approached with Gideon just a step behind. "Lord and ladies, pleasure to make your acquaintance."

The man nodded and looked to Gideon who stepped forward and also bowed at the waist. "Thank you for your gracious invitation."

Lord Monroe's hooded eyes roved over them and he gave them a slight nod. "May I present my wife, Lady Fern Monroe, and my daughter, Prudence."

The women both nodded, the older one smiling up at them in a way that didn't quite convey warmth. "Welcome to our home. Please sit." She rang a bell and two maids appeared with trays.

"I do hope you enjoy brandy," Lord Monroe said as the maids lowered a tray in front of both of them. "My own, made here on the estate. I normally serve spirits made locally," he added.

It was hard for Camren not to exchange a look with Gideon at the slight. Camren sipped the liquid and found it lacking. When he noticed Lord Monroe's pointed look, he took a second. "It is quite good."

The man's lips curved. "Of course."

Unlike the day before, the Monroes seemed awkward and stilted.

Gideon, who was used to dealing with harder business clients, motioned to the lord. "May I ask about your process to make this brandy?"

Prudence stood and motioned to a balcony. "Would you like some fresh air, Laird?"

Because it would be rude not to accept, Camren got to his feet.

The lord slid a look to Gideon. "Of course, but first I am curious. Tell me, Mister Sutherland, what is the nature of your business here in London?"

They sought to separate them. Camren had full trust in Gideon to speak on behalf of their whisky company, so he followed the waif-thin Prudence out to the balcony.

There was little comparison between this garden and the one he'd sat in the day before. He peered down to see a team of gardeners trimming flowers, working in silence as they pruned, swept and pushed small carts away.

"They should have been done by now," Prudence told him, following his line of sight. "I apologize for their appearance." She grimaced. "My mother will be most cross upon finding out."

"In Scotland, I do not mind seeing my staff and villagers about. People who work are valuable."

"Indeed," Prudence replied, not seeming in the slightest convinced. "I hear you called on my cousin yesterday," she added, catching him off guard.

He frowned. "You are related to Evangeline Prescott?"

"Yes, her mother and mine are sisters. They are very different, as you are well aware, my mother taking after their father who had darker coloring."

Unsure what to say, he remained silent. Prudence resembled her mother in hair color but had her father's colorless pale skin. A most unfortunate combination.

"I hope I am not overstepping by warning that you must keep your distance from my poor dear cousin. She is not someone to be associated with if you wish to gain business within London's polite society."

"I consider myself forewarned." He hoped to change the subject. Not that he felt any kind of loyalty to Evangeline, but Camren hated gossip. Especially when masked as a friendly warning.

Prudence placed a pale hand on his forearm and leaned forward, ensuring he had a clear view down the front of her bodice. Although well endowed, her almost transparent skin did little to affect him. Instead, his mind wandered to how much he'd enjoyed the glimpse of Evangeline's bust.

"Her fall from grace was more of a foolish, headfirst dive that left her ruined forever. The sad thing is, it was all her own doing." She lowered her voice to a whisper. "I feel it is my duty to let you know she was caught bereft of clothing with a man, in public."

When he remained silent, she added, "Her penchant for seducing men was well known, however they remained whispers out of respect for my aunt and uncle. My heart breaks that because of her affliction that sent her to such extremes it caused my aunt and uncle to be utterly humiliated."

"They seem to be doing well," he had to say, feeling a need to speak up for the Prescotts. "I enjoyed my visit with them very much."

Prudence's face hardened. "I am glad to hear it." She looked to the doorway and managed to move closer, their bodies almost touching. "If I may be forward and ask, Laird. Do you plan to marry her and chance taking a promiscuous woman back to your home in Scotland?"

"Miss Prudence, your mother requests your presence," interrupted a maid. The maid's gaze pinned the spot where Prudence's hand lay on his arm before turning and walking back inside.

"Shall we?" Camren asked, motioning to the doors, relieved to put space between them.

Once inside, the conversation was redirected to his and Gideon's plans for their stay in London.

"I must insist you both attend the gala next week," Lady Monroe said. "Everyone looks forward to our spring ball with much anticipation."

"Of course, you must," Lord Monroe added before taking a bite of food. His demeanor, that of someone who preferred to be anywhere rather than there, was quite comical.

There was barely a spare inch on the table between platters of roasted duck, meat pies, puddings and platters of steaming vegetables of several types. Camren wondered why the family was trying so hard to impress him. There was little he could do for a family of such high standing.

Camren decided it was best to wait until conferring with Gideon before accepting the invitation. However, it was probable he would have a hard time finding an excuse.

"I will save you a spot in my dance card," Prudence said, her eyes locked on his. "I would think a man from Scotland would be a great dancer."

"Aye, he is," Gideon said, "but I am sure you're aware he is recently betrothed."

The statement seemed to interest Lord Monroe whose eyes narrowed in his direction. "Is this true?" He looked to both his wife and daughter as if they held some sort of say in the matter. "I wasn't aware."

Lady Monroe waved a dismissive hand. "The work of Mrs. Dove-Lyon. I wouldn't call it set in stone."

It began to dawn on Camren that the Monroes considered him a potential suitor for their daughter. His blood ran cold. Somehow, he would have to get out of the situation without making enemies.

"What of you, Mr. Sutherland?" Lady Monroe asked, eyes narrowed. "Have you been caught up in such an outrageous manner as well?"

When he slid a look to Gideon who sat across the table from him, his friend scowled down at his food before looking to the woman. "No. I plan to marry a Scottish woman."

"I see." Lady Monroe's reply was curt. She lifted a bell and rang it.

Camren started at a hand resting on his upper leg and sliding toward his inner thigh. He cleared his throat and slid at look at Prudence who looked the picture of innocence, her gaze forward. At the same time, four servants entered, two empty-handed and two with laden trays.

There was little he could do. Standing was out of the question so he remained frozen in place as his plate was cleared and replaced with a smaller one that held a slice of fruit tart.

Everyone ate very little, most of the food was left and he wondered again what the reason for the invitation was. "Lord Monroe, I appreciate your generous invitation to partake in this delicious meal. If there is anything you and your family require of us, please let us know."

"This is for social pleasure only, I assure you," Lord Monroe replied. "Mr. Sutherland made me aware of the reason for your being in London. Although I have an extensive reach in London society, I rarely use it."

When the man paused, obviously waiting for them to plead their case, Camren forced a pleasant tone. "I can certainly understand."

An awkward silence followed as, no doubt, Lord Monroe waited for them to ask for his assistance, which neither Gideon nor he would do.

"Well," Lady Monroe finally said. "Should we go to the sitting room?"

No one had touched their tart with the exception of Gideon. He'd speared it, lifted it, sniffed it and put it back down.

Glad to escape Prudence's meandering touch, Camren was the first to stand.

The men followed the women out of the dining room to the sitting room.

Lord Monroe and Gideon settled into chairs, while Camren went to stand by the hearth, feigning interest in a dull painting over it.

"Tell us about your home, Laird," Lady Monroe said.

He hesitated as servants entered and poured sherry. Although he, too, had staff, he always poured drinks for his visitors. The Prescotts had done the same.

"My main family keep is about double the size of this home. However, I house many people there. My mother, two brothers, an elderly aunt and several of my guards live there. Clan Maclean holdings includes two large villages and five farms."

Gideon became animated, adding, "Clan Maclean boasts over five hundred warriors and archers that protect the clan and our allies from encroachment." He motioned to Camren. "Do not forget the other homes, the smaller Maclean keep and house where your uncle, Calum, lives."

It was obvious that Gideon had noticed that the family was doing their best to impress, so he did the same in return.

"We have a country estate that is quite large, as well," Prudence interjected, raising her nose into the air. "However, I am not keen on country life. I prefer the excitement and vibrance of London."

Camren looked to her. "I am afraid you would not care for Highland life then, Miss Monroe."

For a moment, she seemed taken aback by his comment, but then smiled. "Oh, I am sure life can be interesting there, as well."

By the time he and Gideon were able to extricate themselves from the Monroes, the sun was setting. Upon climbing into the carriage, both let out long breaths.

"That was positively painful," Gideon said. "I wish there was a bottle of whisky in here." He looked around just to be sure.

Camren closed his eyes. "I hope they do not pursue the idea of either one of us marrying that woman."

Gideon shook his head. "I am going to sell the property I won straightaway. Since winning it, I've received numerous invitations to call on people I have no desire to meet."

"We could move there for the rest of the season and sell it just before returning to Scotland," Camren suggested. "Boasting that address may help our business."

He laughed when Gideon growled in annoyance and leaned forward to speak. "I'd rather return to Scotland unsuccessful than suffer through another evening like this one."

Upon arriving at the townhouse, they both settled into chairs, seeming to have no energy to do much more than breathe.

Daniel appeared with a tray, on it a stack of envelopes. He lifted an eyebrow at Gideon. "Most of these are for you."

"Perhaps we should speak of returning to Scotland?" Gideon asked. "I may leave sooner than you."

Camren was in total agreement with his friend. However, the monetary gains from sales in England had the potential to be vast. Although his own holdings were large, he did wish to help with the many requirements of his clan.

"I have many people that require help. It is my obligation to our clan to ensure they are cared for. Just one more month and we will return."

Gideon grunted. "Being here in London society should be preferable to most things, but I find I'd prefer a battle to being here."

CHAPTER SEVEN

"THERE IS MUCH to do for the wedding." Evangeline's mother hurried into the parlor where she sat, followed by the seamstress. She stopped and gave her daughter a sharp look. "Honestly, Evangeline, should you not be doing something other than reading?"

A dress had already been chosen, most of her clothing packed. Several trunks with her belongings lined the hallway upstairs.

"The marriage is not to take place for another five days, if we count today." She stretched. "A lot can happen in five days."

"Four days," her mother corrected. "Mrs. Langley is delivering the last of the gowns I ordered. Gowns made from thicker fabric since life in Scotland could be rather harsh in the winter."

At her mother's sniff, Evangeline felt her own chest constrict. "Why did it have to be someone who lives so far?"

"I didn't suspect he'd be the one," her mother confessed. "I also chose Lord Whitaker, knowing his sharp mind and wit would be compatible with yours."

Evangeline fought the urge to shudder. Although attractive, Lloyd Whitaker was too young and a bit feminine in her opinion. "Mother, you are not a good matchmaker."

The seamstress motioned for two young women to enter. Both had gowns over their arms. It would be an entire morning before they were done.

"Laird Maclean is to come this afternoon," her mother said. "He's requested to take you on a carriage ride."

Shivers of awareness rushed through her and, immediately, the last time she'd ridden in a carriage with a man came to mind.

"I'd prefer not to."

"We've already accepted," her mother replied. "I took the liberty of replying for you."

Hours later, Evangeline trudged to her room after the seamstress left. A messenger had arrived with several invitations for her and her mother to attend tea the following afternoon. The only reason for the invitations was obviously fodder for gossip.

The only one they accepted was to visit the Edwards' home, since Rose and her family would be one of the few guests at the marriage ceremony.

Although a message had been sent to her sister, Priscilla, it was not probable they'd have enough time to travel and attend.

"I have yet to find a way out of this," Evangeline said out loud. "Whatever can I do?"

Fran hurried in. "I'm sorry, Miss Genie. I was detained in the kitchen. Sit so I can comb your hair."

"No need," Evangeline replied. "I did it myself. Come sit," she said as she patted a chair next to her. "You must tell me everything you've heard about my situation."

Fran bit her bottom lip and looked to the side. "Most of it is not agreeable in the least, Miss."

"It cannot be worse than what's been said in the past." Her stomach tightened with the familiar ache since her fall from grace. "Tell me."

"Well," Fran started. "First of all, everyone is scrambling to find out the reason Laird Maclean would propose. They suspect you and he... well that you are with child."

Evangeline rolled her eyes. "That is not as bad as I'd think. There must be more."

"Some say that the laird is indebted to your father and was forced into it."

As much as she wanted to know, at the same time it was horrible how the people she'd once counted as friends seemed to relish ways to say bad things about her. At one time, she'd been the toast of London society. She supposed, in a way, she still was, giving them much for conversations over drinks.

"What else?"

At Fran's hesitation, Evangeline prepared herself to hear something truly hurtful. "Laird Maclean called on Miss. Prudence. Susy said they were quite intimate when she walked in on them," Fran continued, referring to her cousin's maid.

Her eyes flew wide. "When?"

"Yesterday. He remained at the Monroe estate until quite late. Susy also inferred that Laird Maclean initiated a walk about the garden to be alone with Miss Prudence."

It was not surprising that Prudence would find a way to spend time with Camren. There was an underlying reason for it. Besides the fact that Camren was a handsome and eligible bachelor, Prudence would find a way to repay what she considered a betrayal. Both she and Prudence had been enamored with Avery Hamilton, but it had been Evangeline he'd chosen to pursue.

Prudence had never forgotten, often accusing Evangeline of stealing him away despite the fact Avery had never once called on her.

"Was anything else said?" she asked in a flat voice.

Fran studied her for a moment. "There is nothing more of note. Most comments were unkind, but the vicar's wife did say that she is glad to hear you will be married off and kept from any more convictions."

"She is kind," Evangeline said and wiped an errant tear. "This entire situation has brought back what happened in the past. I wish Mother would have listened to me and not gone forward with this ridiculous notion. Laird Maclean is not the least bit interested in marrying me, I'm sure."

WHEN THE FOOTMAN announced Camren Maclean's arrival minutes later, and he strode into the sitting room, Evangeline did her best to keep her heart from pounding. Part of her reaction was his appearance.

Wearing the fashion of the time, he still managed to look every bit a Scot. Unlike most Englishmen, his olive skin and sun-bleached hair were testament to the hours spent outdoors.

"Miss Prescott," he said as he bowed over her hand and then placed it in the crook of his arm. "Shall we proceed?"

"I must speak to you." Evangeline attempted to pull back, but he held her fast. "You may change your mind about..."

He pinned her with a knowing look. "We can speak in the carriage. I am tired of being indoors and it is a beautiful day." It was an open carriage which allowed for everyone to see them. Not particularly what Evangeline wished for at the moment.

"Can we avoid Hyde Park?"

"I had not planned to go there."

For the first few minutes, they rode in silence. It wasn't awkward, more of a time to gain their bearings. Camren reached for a basket on the bench opposite them. "Would you like some wine?"

"If I am to be honest, I'd prefer something stronger," Evangeline replied with a grimace. "I have much to tell you."

From a flask in the basket, he poured them each whisky and settled back against the plush seat. "I find this mode of travel rather interesting," he began. "I am not used to going anywhere unless on horseback. On occasion, I drive a loaded wagon, but it is rare."

After a sip of her drink, she studied the view for a moment, allowing the warmth of the whisky to flow down her throat. "I imagine the surroundings are much more beautiful where you are from."

"The city has it's qualities," he replied. Although if he were to be honest, most of the time he found the views lacking.

"You are being generous," Evangeline replied. "When I visit the country estate, I can spend hours riding. Just the freshness of the air alone is wonderful."

When she found him studying her intently, she took another sip of whisky. "I hear you visited with my cousin."

Camren nodded. "I did."

"And I imagine she did not hesitate to give you the details of my ruin."

"I would rather hear it from you, Miss Prescott. If we are to be married, I prefer only honesty between us. Tell me."

Was it what she wished for? If anything, she'd expected him to call off the wedding after speaking to Prudence. Her cousin had probably not only informed him of her fall from grace but had embellished freely.

The marriage had to be called off. Not because she wasn't attracted to him, but because she did not wish him to be saddled with a ruined woman with a physical impediment.

"I was young and quite foolish. My actions on that day were wrong, and I carry the consequences with each step. My leg injury is a permanent reminder of my fall from grace."

His face hardened. "You do not say to be regretful."

"Of course, I am."

"For the betrayal or for being caught?"

Her breath caught. "Betrayal?" Of course, Prudence must have intimated that Avery was her suitor.

"I believe the gentleman in question was your cousin's..."

"He was not."

The air around them seemed to still and Evangeline wished Camren would have listened to her and not insisted on going out.

They rode down cobblestone streets to the outskirts of the city until they had a view of more open areas between large estates. The crisp air flowed around them for which Evangeline was thankful. She'd stopped talking, needing time to organize her thoughts.

In the meantime, Camren sipped his drink and poured a second. There was a shift in him, as if a wall were erected between them that had not been there, at least not to her the day he'd first visited.

"Why would your cousin accuse you of something that is not true?" he asked, his face devoid of expression.

Every explanation on the tip of her tongue sounded more ludicrous than the next. Up until that day, she'd considered their rivalry something in the past, a misunderstanding of two young, emotional girls.

She met Camren's gaze. "Before he became my suitor, Prudence and I shared an admiration for him. I suppose she is still bitter over the fact he chose me."

"I see." It was hard to tell if he was convinced or not, but he did seem to relax.

"To be clear, Laird, I will not fret if you believe me or not. You asked that we be honest with each other and I, too, prefer it."

"It's good to hear." Camren leaned closer, his lips to her ear. "I must admit feeling a great attraction to you, Miss Prescott. I can certainly understand why a man would choose you." The caress of his warm breath against her sensitive skin caused an immediate urgent reaction. Her breath caught and her eyelids fell closed. It had been so very long since she'd had a man so close.

"I-I..." Words evaded her at the touch of his lips to just below her jawline.

He pressed a kiss to her jaw. It was soft, almost hesitant.

Evangeline swallowed and turned to study the placid expression on his face. Nothing came to mind. She could not think of a thing to say.

If only this once, she had to know what it would be like to kiss him. A plan was already formulating, a way to avoid marriage. Although if she were to be honest, he was probably the very type of man she would not mind being bound to.

However, the sordid details of her past had reared on the lips of London society and surely would reach the ears of Camren's family even before they arrived.

Her gaze moved to his lips, with an unspoken request. Camren responded and his mouth covered hers.

Without thought, she cupped his face with her right hand. His face was smooth, the skin warm under her fingertips. Fiery awareness trickled through her veins to pool in the most delicate part of her. How could a simple kiss cause such a reaction?

Longing made her want to demand more from him, but at the carriage going over a rough patch and swaying side-to-side, reality crept ever so slowly into her muddled brain.

His hand was now at her waist. His fingers pressed into the fabric and, for a brief moment, Evangeline imagined them touching her bare skin.

"I am not sure what came over me." She placed her hand against his chest and gently pushed him back. "We must speak. How do you feel about our situation?"

His darkened gaze moved over her face and then away to the scenery passing by. "I am prepared to go forth with the marriage. I have given my word. However, I must make it clear that I will never tolerate infidelity."

If only the ground would open and pull her into its darkened depths. Heat rushed to her face and her eyes burned as she turned away to stare blindly at the road before them. Of all the humiliations since the incident, his pronouncement felt like a stab through her heart.

The sheer embarrassment of being considered a harlot was enough to make her want to jump from the moving carriage. Instead, she closed her eyes and forced the bile that threated to erupt from her back down.

"If I ever marry, my entire body and soul will belong to my husband. However, Laird, you do not know me, and I find your remark insulting. You have no reason to trust me and I understand that. Despite what my cousin may have alluded to, I was faithful to the one man who was my lover and he was never her suitor."

"I am not alluding to anything other than making a statement to the matter of our future relationship. We will be married, Miss Prescott, and I do expect fidelity and I vow to be faithful to you as well. My first marriage ended because of a lack of it."

Her eyes widened. Of course, it made the current situation even worse. Not only did he have doubts about her, but the entire situation was probably a stark reminder of what had happened.

"I understand," Evangeline replied. In truth, she was sure he would not have made the remark as strongly if she were anyone else. Someone who was not scorned by society for promiscuity.

Just then, a rider appeared in the distance. The silver-hued stallion was familiar, and she narrowed her eyes, attempting to get a clearer view.

The rider sat tall in his saddle, the familiar figure moving closer until there was no question of his identity.

Evangeline's blood ran cold.

Approaching at a rapid pace was Avery Hamilton, the man who'd played a major part in the ruin of her reputation.

He seemed intent on coming toward them, so much so that Camren ordered their carriage to stop.

Avery's dark gaze surveyed Evangeline for a long moment before sliding to Camren. "Good afternoon, Evangeline." He cocked an eyebrow and waited to be introduced.

Without any alternative, she let out a breath. "Avery, I introduce Laird Camren Maclean. Camren, this is Lord Avery Hamilton. A family acquaintance."

The men exchanged a slight bow of their heads, neither breaking eye contact. Neither ceded until Evangeline interrupted.

"Have a good day, Avery."

The lord's gaze swept from her face, past Camren and to the driver. "I am glad to see you are venturing out again." With that, he touched the brim of his hat and rode away.

Evangeline sat still, her gaze straight ahead. If only the infernal day would end.

THE BELL OVER the door at The Tattered Page dinged as a she entered. Prudence sniffed at the unpleasant smell of books and dust, both left on the shelf much too long. Her day was going well. Already, she'd sent Avery Hamilton on a fool's errand and now to find out information to further humiliate the harlot cousin of hers.

Behind the counter was a man she assumed to be in his midthirties. He wasn't too unpleasant to look upon, although it was definitely not someone she should notice. He was definitely a poor man, with little more than the tidy shop.

"May I help you, Miss?" His brown gaze fell on her for an instant.

"I am looking for my cousin, Evangeline. Is she here?"

He seemed surprised at her question. "No, Miss. Her book club meets on Wednesday mornings."

"Goodness." She feigned confusion. "Why did I think she said today? What time is the book club held?"

"They begin at ten and are normally done by noon." He studied her. "Should I tell her to expect you?"

"No, no, please don't. I wish to surprise her." Prudence hurried back out without a backward glance.

CHAPTER EIGHT

T HE EVENING OF the ball arrived, and Evangeline had run out of excuses not to attend. Now, she found herself in a carriage headed to what she was sure would be another unpleasant event.

The ride to the ball was surreal. Evangeline didn't speak as she absorbed the fact that she was in a carriage with Camren and his friend, Gideon, being chaperoned by Martha.

Usually, she would ride with her parents and quickly find a quiet corner upon arriving at the ball without escort. Tonight, her entrance was not to be anything like before.

As a betrothed couple, especially being Camren was titled, it was expected they'd enter together. This was to be their first social appearance and Evangeline's stomach was in knots. The last thing she wished for was to limp into a room on the arm of London's talk of the town.

She slid a look to Camren who spoke with Gideon of an earlier business meeting. Sensing her perusal, he looked to her. "I hear your aunt and uncle expect important families to be in attendance. I hope you do not mind that Gideon and I plan to make acquaintances that could assist our business."

"Of course not. That is what most men do at these functions." She gave him a reassuring smile. "The women come to show off for each other and the men to make connections."

Gideon nodded. "As much as I dislike social functions, it is the best place for business talks."

Evangeline let out a sigh. "Personally, I am not fond of them, either. I prefer to sit and watch the goings-on. What about you, Camren?"

Lifting and lowering his left shoulder, his lips curved. "I've always liked social functions in Scotland. The gatherings always provide plenty of entertainment. Gay music and cheerful conversations are enjoyable in my opinion." What he described was utterly different than a ball at her aunt and uncle's home.

Too soon, the carriage pulled up to the Monroe estate. Evangeline did her best to calm her thudding heart, but it was difficult. Every eye would be on her and Camren. The whispers and commentary, however dreadful, would eventually reach her ears. How would Camren deal with the horrible side of London society? He was, in all probability, not used to it. In Scotland, rules were much more relaxed and although she was sure there was still gossip, society was not as rigid. Women had more freedoms in Scotland and were not encumbered by such stringent rules.

When the carriage came to a stop, a footman opened the door and stood back, holding the door open. First, Gideon stepped out, followed by Camren who assisted her down. Martha would remain with the carriage and be taken to a secondary location where the servants would hold a gathering of their own while waiting to be called to return to their homes with their employers.

Evangeline turned and looked back to Martha who gave her a warm reassuring smile. "Enjoy yourself, Miss."

Doing her best to maintain a pleasant expression, she placed her hand in the crook of Camren's arm and walked beside him up the steps and into the ballroom.

The ballroom glowed and music wafted from the open doorways out to the darkening evening. The voices of those already gathered ebbed and flowed almost in a rhythmic pattern. Each wave of sound hit Evangeline like a punch to her stomach.

She pulled back and Camren stopped. "What is wrong? Am I walking too fast?"

"No. I'm sorry. It's just that I'm a bit nervous about walking inside. Everyone will talk."

"They will," he replied matter-of-factly. "What they say or do has little to do with us. People are who they are and those easily influenced by others, we should pity."

His logic made sense. "You are correct, but it doesn't help me feel any more at ease."

"Let us be brave." He continued forth until they arrived just inside the doorway. The butler announced their names, and many heads swiveled in their direction. Evangeline walked beside Camren, head held high, gaze forward. Admittedly, she walked on her right toes to keep from limping.

Her uncle, aunt and Prudence were lined up to greet them. Camren spoke for Evangeline and Gideon when greeting the trio. As usual, her uncle, Lord Monroe, was pale and without expression, his cold eyes moving from Camren to her. "Nice to see you in attendance, dear niece." He pressed a light kiss to her jaw, which always surprised her. He'd always been kind and seemed to have a soft spot for her.

As per usual, her aunt and Prudence only had eyes for Camren and Gideon. They fawned over the men as if they were royalty, pretending to talk of private conversations they'd held.

"Darling, you look beautiful," Lady Monroe said and then ruined her greeting with the next statement. "If you become overly tired of standing, there are chairs against the walls." Her aunt pointed across the room even though a group of chairs were right beside them.

It was hard not to glare, but Evangeline managed a slight smile. "Your caring for my well-being is lovely, dear aunt. I am fine to stand."

Prudence gave her a wan smile. "Where are Uncle Forest and Aunt Olivia? I am shocked they'd allow you in a carriage alone with a man."

"We had a chaperone," Camren replied. "I would not take liberties with my betrothed."

Put in her place, Prudence's face fell, but she recovered quickly. "Of course, *you* would not," she replied, pinning Camren with an innocent look and emphasizing the word "you".

Evangeline could have cried in relief when Rose, Harriett and Ramona approached to greet her.

The women were introduced to Camren and Gideon and, quickly, along with Camren and Gideon, they made their way to the opposite side of the ballroom.

They remained for a while, Evangeline's parents joining them soon after. A footman brought chairs, no doubt sent by her aunt or cousin just to prove a point. Camren and Gideon excused themselves and went with her father to be introduced to some business acquaintances.

Rose met Evangeline's gaze. "What is he like? Does he take your breath away?"

She had to smile at her friend's cheerful disposition. It was nice to be treated normally. "He is a bit on the stern side, but quite nice."

"His friend, Gideon, is quite handsome, isn't he? I wonder who will be throwing daughters in his face."

Their mothers whispered to each other, their eyes darting toward the other side of the ballroom.

Rose grimaced. "Ever since your mother decided you should be married off, mine is beginning to plot against me, as well."

"I wish you luck," Evangeline replied. "I am still trying to figure out how to get out of my current predicament. I do not wish to leave London married to a man who was tricked into marrying me."

A servant neared with a tray of lukewarm punch and they each took a glass. It would only become hotter in the room when more people arrived, so it was best to drink something.

"Oh, no. He's here," Rose said, her eyes darting to the entrance.

Avery Hamilton entered, accompanied by another gentleman who Evangeline recognized as his good friend. Automatically, every eye moved from him to her and then back. Evangeline pretended not to notice but was sure her face pinkened. Would the gossips ever let what happened go?

Unlike her, Avery did not seem at all bothered by the attention. He was welcomed by the hosts and was warmly greeted by Prudence who made a show of laughing overly loud at something he said.

Evangeline clenched her back teeth in annoyance. "Why do I have to be related to her?"

"And why do we come here every year?" Rose added.

Being that they were related to the hosts, it would be considered a social affront for her family not to attend. She and her parents had bravely faced people just a year after her fall from grace at the Monroe ball and now, three years later, it was clear nothing was forgotten.

Admittedly, her aunt and uncle had never changed the manner in which they treated her. Her uncle was as warm as he could be when seeing her and her aunt would point out obvious things, not thinking how the words sounded. Prudence, however, took delight in reminding her of what had happened in different, cunning ways.

The music began and couples lined up and began familiar dances. Evangeline couldn't help but smile as she watched the flow of the wide skirts and movements of the gentlemen's feet as they went through the paces. Everyone was dressed beautifully, the colors making the dance look even more lovely.

She stood with Rose to watch the dancers. Camren joined them. His presence gave her a constant sense of security and protection. No one dared to look at her in a judgmental manner with the imposing

Scotsman at her side.

"Would you like to dance?" he asked when the next song began.

She shook her head. "I feel self-conscious, so I prefer not to."

"I understand," he replied.

"Do you like to dance?" Evangeline asked, trying to picture him moving about a dance floor.

His lips curved just a bit. "Not particularly. My mother taught us to dance and ensured we could move about the dance floor without stepping on anyone's toes. But my brothers and I would prefer to do a jig to this." He motioned to the dance floor as the couples began a waltz.

Evangeline giggled. "I can only imagine how distressful it was for your poor mother."

ROSE TRIED TO figure out what to do with her punch. It was annoying to hold the empty cup and no one coming to collect it. With Camren and Evangeline next to her, she felt like a frumpy chaperone. Although she would like to dance, most of the men present were being ushered to the younger, unmarried women in the room.

She understood and wondered, once again, why she'd not accepted any of the suitors who'd come calling years earlier. Instead, like a ninny, she'd held out hope for one man. And now said man danced with his wife, whom he'd already fathered two children with.

A sigh escaped and she turned her attention in a different direction only to have her gaze fall upon Gideon. Lady Winters and her two daughters surrounded him. The women's fans moved as fast as their lips, each placing a hand on his forearm when speaking.

His Adam's apple bobbed, and he leaned back just a bit. Every time he took a slight step backward, the trio of women moved with him.

Rose felt bad for him. If he was not used to London society, it would be a hard season for the poor man. She was not sure what possessed her, but she placed her cup on a table and walked directly to the group. She smiled politely at the women.

"I am so very sorry to interrupt. But I do believe Mister Sutherland owes me this dance."

Lady Winters' eyes bulged. "Rose, one should wait for the gentleman to come to you."

"If he can, but he was detained," Rose snapped and placed her hand in the crook of Gideon's arm. "The song would have been over before he'd make it to where I was."

Lady Winters gasped and looked to her daughters who seemed in a trance and continued to bat their lashes at Gideon.

"I don't know if I should thank you or warn you," Gideon said as they walked away. "I am not much of a dancer."

"Neither am I," Rose replied. "I prefer to play music than dance to it."

On the dance floor, they managed a waltz. It was not the best dance, but both worked hard not to stumble or step on one another's feet. Rose failed more than Gideon. When it was over, he guided her back to where Evangeline and Camren were standing.

"That was rather painful to watch," Evangeline told her with a giggle. "What possessed you to dance?"

"She saved my life," Gideon interjected before Rose could reply. "In payment, I danced with her. I never dance."

"That is true," Camren said with a surprised expression. "He detests it. I hope he apologized for your feet," he added.

Rose giggled. "I believe we both failed in that."

When Gideon moved closer, Rose's stomach clenched. She'd been so intent on dancing correctly that she'd not considered she'd just danced with a very handsome man who made her feel things considered long dormant.

"Thank you for the dance." His green eyes twinkled. "This is the first time a woman has save me from peril. I am forever in your debt."

Doing her best to temper the butterflies in her stomach, she gave him what she hoped was a bland look. "You are my best friend's betrothed's friend. It is the least I could do."

EVERYWHERE EVANGELINE LOOKED, people whispered and watched her. When her uncle approached, she was somewhat glad for the interruption. As much as she was glad for Camren's presence, the constant perusal of the people in the room was tiring.

"There is someone I'd like to introduce you to," her uncle said and both Camren and Gideon went to where a group of older gentlemen were gathered.

Evangeline nudged Rose. "What possessed you to do it? It was rather comical to see two people who can't dance try to."

"Imagine being the one dancing," Rose replied with a shake of her head. "I felt bad for him. Seeing he was surrounded by Mrs. Winters and her two awkward daughters, I rescued him only to put him in peril of losing a toe."

They chuckled lightly. "I will go get punch," Rose said, leaving her alone.

Evangeline took several steps closer to open doors to get fresh air. Outside, the balcony was empty. Once Rose returned, they would go out.

"You look lovely this evening." Avery's voice fell over her like ice water.

This could not be happening. Since the unfortunate event, he'd never dared to speak to her again, especially not in public. With every thud of her heart, she scanned the room for Rose or her mother.

Rose was being held back by an older woman and her mother was nowhere to be seen. In a desperate attempt to get away from prying eyes, she rushed out to the balcony.

"Get away from me. I do not wish to speak to you. What are you thinking?" Every statement she spoke in a desperate hushed tone made her angrier.

"I would not have come to speak to you. However, your cousin said you had something important to tell me."

Of course, Prudence would find a way to attempt to ruin her engagement.

"Prudence is only out to cause me problems. I have nothing to say to you, Avery."

His eyes roamed over her body. "You are ravishing, as always. I have thought about our times together often and must admit to missing you."

"Please go. Your words are ridiculous."

He nodded, looking down. "I owe you so many apologies."

"They are not accepted, go away."

Avery let out a long sigh. "This Scotsman is a lucky man. I am sure he has enjoyed your adventurous nature."

"Leave." Evangeline turned away, her breath coming in short gasps. She would make excuses and leave immediately. She hoped no one saw her and Avery step out there and was spreading the news to those gathered. She didn't look to see if he left but kept her sights directly out to the gardens. Admittedly, she didn't see anything past the misting of her eyes.

"I wasn't sure where to find you." Camren had appeared while she was looking away. Could the evening get any worse?

She turned to his cold, assessing gaze that moved from her lips to her throat. Did he actually think she'd been out there kissing another man? Evangeline pressed her lips together and curled her fingers into fists.

"I came out to get fresh air. Rose was supposed to bring me punch." She looked up at him.

He slid a glance toward the ballroom. "Did you invite him to join you to gather the air?"

"No, I did not."

Once again, he looked to where Avery had gone. "He seemed

rather fervent about something."

"If you wish to know if I kissed him or plan to meet with him in the garden later for a tryst or perhaps escape in a carriage, just ask me." Fury rose and she fought not to shove Camren aside and run away. Instead, she stood stock still, her body trembling with rage.

In that moment, she wanted Camren to soften and reassure her. Instead, he turned on his heel and walked away.

It was like a slap to the face. Her heart splintered into pieces and she slumped onto the railing.

"Darling, are you all right?" Her mother rushed out. "I just saw Camren and he said you were out here."

She met her mother's worried gaze. "I'm angry. Nothing is wrong. I do wish to go home as I'm sure people will begin to talk soon."

"What happened?"

"Avery was just out here. Prudence set it up."

Her mother's face hardened. "Enough is enough. I am going to speak to her and my sister about this constant need of hers to upset you."

Just then, a scream was followed by a collective gasp. There were loud murmurings as she and her mother hurried to the doorway to see what had happened.

In the center of the room, a woman lay sprawled while another, dressed in rather dower clothing, stood over her with a furious glare. "I have warned you more than once," the woman screamed. "Stay away from my husband, you harlot."

The woman on the floor, was young, the daughter of a prominent banker. The other was not a guest.

A couple of men came and took the interloper away, while the young socialite's parents and another lady picked the girl from the floor and hurried her out.

"The poor dear," her mother said, shaking her head. She looked to Evangeline. "I do not think you will be the center of conversation."

Evangeline searched the ballroom and met Camren's gaze. He looked away, obviously still displeased with whatever idea he'd formed in his head.

"Perhaps it's all for the best. The wedding should be called off, Mother. Camren walked out and saw me with Avery. He is, of course, thinking the worst."

"I will speak to him, as well," her mother said. "However, I do agree. It's best we leave. Tomorrow, I have much to do."

CHAPTER NINE

"I TAKE IT things between you and your fiancée are not well," Gideon said the next morning as Camren prepared to leave to ride and clear his head.

Camren shook his head. "She was quite cross with me and left without letting me know. You had already disappeared. I won't ask where. So, I came back here as soon as I was aware Evangeline and her parents had left to avoid any questions."

"It was quite an event-filled night," Gideon said with a grin. "I was hiding in the carriage for a while to get away from overly exuberant mothers attempting to toss daughters practically into my lap." He chuckled. "I asked Daniel to bring me back and return for you. Didn't he tell you?"

"No. But then again, I was in a dark mood and wasn't in the mood to talk."

MOMENTS LATER, HE rode toward Hyde Park. Evangeline's cousin had asked that he meet her to choose a bride gift, and although he wondered why, it was too late to cancel. He'd excuse himself, not agreeing to spend more than a minute with the woman, as it was obvious she plotted and planned constantly to ensure he and Evangeline's marriage be called off.

Once at the appointed place, he waited for her to arrive.

Across the street, he noticed a bookstore and considered browsing. But it was almost the time he'd agreed to meet with Prudence, so he didn't dare walk away.

"Dear Camren, thank you so much for meeting me. I have an idea for the perfect gift for my cousin." Prudence hesitated and frowned. "Oh, dear, my shoe has become unlaced. Would you be a dear and assist me."

Camren lowered to one knee and motioned for her to put her foot on his other leg and tied the laces. It was a quick task.

"Thank you so much," she cooed in a much too familiar manner. He noted she used his first name, and considered that he and Evangeline had not gotten to that point. "Where do you propose I procure this gift?" He pointed to what looked to be a jewelry shop. It was then he noticed Evangeline and her friend, Rose, walking away from the bookstore. Rose turned and glared at them, then continued on. Evangeline's limp was noticeable as she hurried away with her friend.

When he looked to Prudence, the woman peered into the window of the store they'd been standing in front of. "This little gift shop has some beautiful figurines. She does love cats."

He gave her a droll look. "I would rather choose something else. Thank you for your help." When he took a step away, she nodded with enthusiasm. "Oh, of course. I will go inside and peruse the items. It was nice seeing you, Camren." She and her maid went into the store.

It was best that he catch up with Evangeline. He needed to speak to her and clear things up. Walking away from her the night before had been rude and if he was to marry the woman, it was time they sat down and spoke about everything. He was not used to the way things were done in London society. Why was Evangeline out at a bookstore? Shouldn't she be planning their wedding? Lost in thought, he went to find his horse.

By the time he arrived at the area where Evangeline had gone, both she and Rose were nowhere to be found. Considering she must have gone home, he was about to head in that direction when he noticed the man who'd been on the balcony with Evangeline.

Avery Hamilton was a dandy, dressed in pastel colors in shades that rivaled a little girl's dress. He walked down the sidewalk with a cane under his arm. Several times, he stopped and tipped his hat at people stopping to make small talk.

Just then, Prudence walked out of the gift shop, her maid's hands filled with packages. How had the woman managed to shop for so much so quickly?

Avery neared and spoke to Prudence. At one point, both burst out in laughter, and she placed a hand on his forearm.

Together, with the maid struggling to keep the packages from falling, they headed toward the park.

He had to speak to Evangeline. Other than a business meeting, his day was clear. First, he'd clear his head and then call on her that evening.

"THIS IS THE most horrible thing your cousin has done up to this point." Her mother tapped a fan on her open palm, her brows lowered in anger. The entire ride to the Monroe estate she'd not stopped talking and Evangeline was glad to see her mother was on her side. In a way, she felt bad for Prudence, as one thing her mother rarely did was raise her voice.

"I must call off the wedding," Evangeline said. "It is for the best that Camren and I do not marry. You must agree, Mother."

Her mother gave her a stern look. "We will postpone it for another few days if we must. There is no rush, but you must marry him. He will lose his home here in London if you do not. Mrs. Dove-Lyon was clear on that."

"Can't he just buy it back?"

"It would go into her property holdings and she is not fond of anyone that does not follow through."

Evangeline certainly didn't want Camren to lose his London home but, at the same time, surely he could purchase another. He was wealthy by all accounts. "He lives in Scotland. Why not lease when traveling here?"

"From what I understood, his father purchased the property for the family. It has more than monetary value." Her mother patted Evangeline's hand. "Everything will be fine. Once we speak to your cousin and aunt, we shall proceed with plans for a wedding."

Evangeline looked up to the blue sky. It was an unseasonably warm day and she held up a parasol to block the sun. "This entire thing has been a fiasco since the very start."

AT THE MONROE mansion, Evangeline and her mother were swiftly guided to a sitting room. Her aunt rushed in with an expression of concern. "Did something happen? I did not expect you today. Should you not be planning the wedding?"

Her mother lowered to sit. On her face was a pleased smile. "There is nothing particularly wrong. However, I must speak to Prudence immediately."

"Of course." Lady Monroe turned to a maid. "Let Miss Prudence know we have company."

Tea was brought and served, the entire time her aunt looking between Evangeline and her mother. "Are you well, Evangeline?"

"Yes, thank you, Aunt."

"Has your dress been delivered?"

"Yes, it has."

"Oh, I bet it's lovely."

Her mother replied this time. "She will look beautiful in it."

Evangeline wanted to roll her eyes. The dress was delivered, but she'd refused to try it on in hopes the wedding would be cancelled and she could have it returned.

Prudence entered, her eyes widening upon seeing who was there. Obviously, the maid had not informed her. "Good afternoon, Aunt... Genie." Her eyes darted to her mother.

"This is a... surprise." She moved to a chair furthest from them and sat. "Tea," she said to a maid who came and served.

"What is this about? You have me on pins and needles," her aunt asked.

Evangeline's mother straightened. "It seems Prudence has gone out of her way to cause problems for Genie. First, she told Avery Hamilton that Evangeline wished to speak to him at the ball. He followed her out to the balcony and Camren saw them." She held her hand up when Prudence attempted to interrupt.

"I am not finished." She gave her niece a sharp look. "What were you doing with Camren Maclean in town today? Why did you meet with him across the street from the bookstore after you asked the shopkeeper for the times Evangeline would be there?"

Prudence's face turned an alarming shade of red, her eyes darting from face to face. "I wanted to help him purchase a wedding gift for Genie."

"You met your cousin's fiancé alone?" Lady Monroe placed a hand over her chest and leaned forward. "Why would you do that?"

"I – I didn't mean to cause trouble." Prudence's bottom lip trembled, but her eyes remained dry.

"You are not invited to the wedding, Prudence, and I prefer it if you do not come to call for a bit. I am most unsettled by your actions."

Evangeline's mother stood and looked to her sister. "I am sorry if I upset you, but this is most upsetting to me, as well."

Lady Monroe blinked, her eyes glistening. "Prudence. I am astonished by your actions. Apologize to your aunt and cousin immediately."

Prudence jumped to her feet. "I will not. Why does she always have to steal men from me? I saw Camren first. I even asked that you invite him here for dinner. I am so tired of everyone catering to my deformed cousin."

"Prudence!" Lady Monroe looked about to swoon as Prudence ran from the room. "Accept... my sincerely apologies. I don't know what's come over her."

"It's best we leave." Evangeline and her mother were escorted to the door by a servant as Lady Monroe remained frozen in her chair, eyes forward.

They rode back to their home in silence, her mother shaking her head every once in a while. Evangeline wanted to feel badly for Prudence, but she could not bring herself to. Her cousin was an indulged woman, much too old to do unreasonable things. If anything, she was making a fool out of herself.

Upon arriving at their home, her mother sent the driver off with a message for Camren and another to Mrs. Dove-Lyon asking for the possibility of postponing the marriage for a few days. She cited wishing for family from out of town to be present.

"There," her mother said, walking into the sitting room. "I think this calls for brandy." She poured a small glass and sipped it while Evangeline peered out the windows.

"If the wedding is not postponed, then it will be the day after to-morrow. I should prepare."

Her mother nodded. "Once the messenger returns, we will send invitations out to just a few people. Rose and her parents, your book club friends, and the three families we've already discussed. I am not sure your aunt and uncle will wish to come. I am sure with Prudence not invited they will feel awkward."

"We will send them an invitation nonetheless," Evangeline said. "I'll start writing them. We will just need a date to finish them off."

CHAPTER TEN

C AMREN, ACCOMPANIED BY Gideon, arrived at the Edwards' home later that afternoon to meet the patriarch. Edwards had made a fortune from his high-end furniture store.

Although it was not necessarily the type of business that would invest in large quantities of whisky, Mr. Edwards was well-connected and also planned to purchase a large amount from them.

"This is most tiresome. I am more than prepared to return to Scotland. We have made enough sales that there should be enough monetary gain for years," Gideon grumbled.

Camren studied his friend for a moment. "I agree. Once this marriage situation is done, and we meet the next three clients, we will return to Scotland. I do not wish to prolong our stay."

"So, another two weeks then?"

"Yes, our appointments cannot be changed. The largest purchaser is out of the country and won't return until the end of the month."

"What of your future wife? She may not wish to depart so soon. Leave her family."

Camren had considered that. He wondered if and when the marriage took place what the plan would then be. There was much to discuss and, thankfully, a message had come just before they'd left, inviting him to dinner.

"I have much to discuss with her. We have to clear things up if there is any chance of this marriage not becoming a disaster."

Gideon chuckled. "It is already much more than a disaster, my friend."

It was true, not only because of Evangeline's past, but also her meddling cousin. It was obvious there was no love lost between them. Although it seemed it was Prudence who did her best to hurt Evangeline. He'd never heard Evangeline say a cross word about Prudence.

He let out a sigh and wondered what that night would bring. The woman he was engaged to was beautiful. She seemed to be kind and caring. Although fetching, he would never consider her to be flirty. He'd not seen her do more than glance whenever a man or woman passed.

When the carriage pulled up to the Edwards' home, they were greeted by a cheerful footman. "Good afternoon, gentlemen. Mr. Edwards is expecting you." They followed him to a large parlor.

The sound of a woman laughing caught their attention. Rose and her father were in the room playing chess and she seemed to be teasing him. "You only beat me because you cheated, Sir."

Mr. Edwards chuckled and shook his head. "It is not becoming of a daughter to accuse her father of being dishonest."

"Laird Maclean and Mister Sutherland," the footman announced.

Neither Edwards nor his daughter seemed surprised by their appearance. The father stood to greet him, while Rose remained sitting, her face flushed.

"Welcome. I apologize for our rude behavior, but my daughter has not learned the art of good sportsmanship."

If Camren were to guess, he would say Rose was the same age as he and Gideon. Perhaps a bit younger. With an oval face, auburn hair and bright eyes to match, she was quite pretty. She smiled at them.

"Welcome to our home."

She stood and gently nudged her father. "I will ensure Mother is aware we have company." Both Camren and Gideon bowed slightly as she took her leave.

Camren slid a glance at Gideon, noticing his friend tracked the woman's movements and cleared his throat as warning.

"Please have a seat. I received your delivery and have yet to taste the different whiskies. I thought perhaps to do it when you arrived."

Gideon chuckled. "If you have not eaten, I would advise very small servings."

"I see you must speak from experience," Mr. Edwards replied with a wide grin. "I will heed your warning."

"Nice to see you old chap," Edwards said, his gaze moving to the doorway as Evangeline's father entered. Edwards was as likeable as Evangeline's father was. The men were obviously good friends, which made for the expectation of a good afternoon.

"Camren, I hear you will be joining us for dinner," Mr. Prescott said and then looked to Gideon. "Please, come along. I hear we are being served roasted pork pie. It is one of Martha's best creations."

A servant entered with a tray of thinly sliced meats and cheeses alongside a chunky loaf of bread.

"Perfect," Mr. Edwards announced. "Now to taste."

A few moments later, they were joined by Rose and Mrs. Edwards. The women sat down and were quickly brought into the conversation. They chatted about the upcoming season and asked questions about his and Gideon's lives in Scotland.

Camren noted that Gideon had yet to drink and his lips itched to grin. His friend seemed to be infatuated by the pretty Miss Rose.

"Laird, do you plan to steal my friend away from me soon?" Rose asked. Her voice was pleasant, but her eyes pinned him with a look that told him she was not the least bit happy with him.

"I have to return to Scotland. But I am sure we will come to an agreement so that she can spend time here."

"You are more than welcome to come to Scotland," Gideon blurted.

The lovely Miss Rose blushed and slid a look to her mother. "Did I tell you I caught sight of the laird with Prudence the day of the ball?"

Mrs. Edwards gave Camren a tight smile. "You must be with care. Prudence is willful and doesn't always have the best in mind when it comes to sweet Evangeline."

Gideon stood with the other gentlemen to go to the sideboard. He would give them the information on each of the whiskeys and what flavors to expect.

It was perfect timing since Camren wanted to ask questions of the women present.

"I hope not to be overstepping," Rose said in a low tone. "I know you are aware of Evangeline's past. My friend is a passionate woman, both in love and friendship. Her passion is just as strong when it comes to devotion."

Mrs. Edwards nodded. "What my daughter says is true. You will not want for a more caring wife. She is a treasure. I pray you can see past all the muddle of what society has created to realize it."

"Thank you," Camren replied. "You put my mind at ease."

"How long do you plan to remain in London?" Rose asked, her gaze sliding to where Gideon stood.

"If all goes as planned, until the end of the month." Camren liked Evangeline's friend and at seeing her frown, he quickly added, "What Gideon said is true. I live in a very large keep. There is more than enough room for all of you to visit."

"I most definitely will." Rose's right eyebrow rose. "I must ensure my friend is happy."

Camren nodded and smiled at Evangeline's devoted friend. "I fear the consequences if she is not."

Mrs. Edwards gave him a knowing smile. "I will venture to say that you and Evangeline will be quite happy once you and she get to know each other. I think you'll be quite compatible."

After excusing himself, he joined the other men to discuss business. The entire time, Mrs. Edwards' comment remained forefront in his mind. Would he and Evangeline indeed be a good match?

Evangeline's father looked to him. "Did I overhear that you plan to return to Scotland soon?"

"Yes, as planned. I have much to do back home. The warm weather is our time for farming, livestock sales and also ensuring housing is reinforced and repaired before the winter," Camren explained.

Mr. Prescott frowned. "I imagine your duties are many then."

"Yes," Camren acknowledged. "The warmer weather also brings to light disputes over land and livestock amongst other things. Both good and bad situations that require my attention. Currently, my brother, Ian, and my uncle are handling things in my stead."

"I am glad to hear you have the support of your family."

Gideon lowered to a chair and conversed with the ladies. Once again, Rose's complexion brightened, the soft coloring adding to her beauty. There was little doubt in Camren's mind that Evangeline's friend would be visiting.

On the ride back to the townhouse, Camren considered his family's reaction to his marriage. He'd yet to send a message, preferring to wait until he was married to do so. It was best to ensure the family would be prepared before he appeared with an English bride in tow.

His mother would be curious and very angry with him for it. It was customary for the laird to marry before the clan. He and Evangeline would have a ceremony there and celebrate, however, it would not be the same.

"Gideon?" Camren began. "Do you think it would be preferable for me not to inform my family about the marriage?"

"And surprise them in person? Or do you plan to leave your new wife here?" Gideon gave him an incredulous look.

It took a moment to formulate his thoughts. "No, what I mean, perform a marriage ceremony back in Scotland. Mother would want to be present at my wedding and I don't wish to cause her undue distress."

His friend pondered the information. "It could work."

"Now to convince Miss Prescott."

"You haven't even moved to calling each other by your given names and you are getting married in two days." Gideon shook his head.

"If it comes to pass, I will make sure to call her Evangeline." Camren laughed. "Or perhaps a pet name of sorts."

WHEN THE BUTLER announced Camren and Gideon's arrival, Evangeline's stomach flipped. Her pulse raced and anger immediately replaced her good mood. He'd insulted her and was now welcomed into her home. If not for the fact that he was her presumed fiancé, she would have refused to see him.

She remained alone in the sitting room. Her mother and father had agreed it was best they speak alone and clear the air before any permanent decisions were made.

Either the marriage would be postponed, or they'd find a way for it not to occur at all. Either way, this evening, things would be resolved between her and Camren. At least that was what she hoped.

The doors opened and Camren stepped in. At seeing him, Evangeline got to her feet. Preferring to stand so that he would not tower over her was her first thought. However, when he neared, she realized how silly the notion was.

He leaned forward and pressed a kiss to her cheek, surprising her.

The press of his warm lips sent her senses reeling, the anger evaporating for an instant.

The kiss was a forward liberty and she wanted to chastise him for it, but instead she let out a shaky breath. "We must talk. There is much to discuss."

He took her hand and held it in both of his. When the hazel gaze met hers, uncertainly and sincerity emanated. "I pray you will forgive my actions at the ball. I was utterly disrespectful to you and treated you in a horrible manner. I can hardly forgive myself for it." Camren lifted her hand and kissed the back of it. "Will you accept my apology?"

"Is that what you think of me? That I will pounce on any opportunity and be frivolously unrestrained when it comes to men?"

Immediately, he shook his head. "No, I do not. I was taken aback and will honestly tell you that I allowed the wrong influence to tamper with my thoughts."

Evangeline was surprised to hear him admit to being influenced. Most men would never admit to someone causing them to do things. Despite his admission, she could not shake the tightness in her chest.

"My past will always affect how people think of me. I have accepted it. However, I can't marry you if, in the back of your mind, you will have doubts. That is why I must ask that we cancel the wedding. We can find a way to ensure your London home remains in the family. Perhaps if the blame is put squarely on me."

He studied her for a long time, making Evangeline wonder what he was thinking.

"I want to marry you, Evangeline."

It was the first time he'd said her name. It sounded perfect, as if he had renamed her. As she sat transfixed, Camren's mouth closed over hers. He tasted of whisky and promise. Her eyelids fell of their own accord.

The attraction between them was without constraint. Evangeline knew full well lovemaking with him would be an explosion of the senses.

She raked her fingers through his hair, acknowledging acceptance and, perhaps, forgiveness. The thought of not exploring more of the man, of not being with him saddened her.

When he pulled her against his chest, she gave in and wrapped her arms around his neck, not caring in that moment if anyone entered. The world disappeared when he deepened the kiss, sending her entire being to shudder with want.

Evangeline moaned against his mouth and Camren responded by trailing kisses down the side of her throat. She wanted more, needed more. It had been much too long that her blood burned like in that moment.

"Oh," she exclaimed when the tip of Camren's tongue made circles at the base of her throat. His breath fanning over the most sensitive skin causing the most sensual of sensations.

Although she became fully aware that his hand slid up from her waist to cup her breast, Evangeline was helpless to speak. Like a plump fruit, he scooped her left breast from its confines and suckled at the pert tip.

Evangeline ran her hand from the back of his head down to his broad back as heat pooled in the center of her core. Just a bit more and she'd come undone. Evangeline was sure of it.

Gently, he returned her breast to its proper place, lifted his head and once again took her mouth. This time, the kiss was lighter.

His gaze delved into hers. "Yes, we should definitely talk."

Camren took Evangeline by the shoulders and peered into her eyes. "I gave my word and I will marry you, Evangeline. And I will strive to be a good husband. From this moment, I will trust you and not consider anything from your past. Can you accept it and be my wife?"

Doubts reared, but at the same time, she could find no fault in his words. He accepted her as she was and would do his best by her. She nodded. "Yes."

His lips curved and his gaze trailed to her lips and then to her breasts. "I cannot wait to be with you. You are breathtaking."

Admittedly, she felt the same way. However, it would be unbecoming to state it out loud. All the rules of polite society had always been so stifling and, in a way, she looked forward to living in a country where things were a bit less strict.

It was evident his chest was wide, and she wondered if there was a dusting of hair on it. Evangeline itched to run her nails down his back and cup his well-formed backside. Oh, and his legs were delightfully muscled. She let out a sigh.

"You are thinking something?" he teased, and she couldn't help but smile back.

"Yes, I am thinking of a response. However, everything I'm thinking should not be spoken out loud."

He leaned toward her and pressed his ear to her mouth. "Whisper your thoughts to me."

Closing her eyes, she first pressed a soft kiss to the soft flesh and then chuckled. "Very well. I imagined what you look like bereft of clothing. The feel of your skin against mine. What your weight will feel like over me." Evangeline hesitated when his breath caught.

"Continue," he said.

"I will not," she whispered. "The rest I will keep to myself."

Camren chuckled and, for a few seconds, kept his head next to hers. He smelled of expensive soap and a bit of leather. She inhaled his scent and he straightened. "Someone is coming."

The door was slightly open, but he blocked her from the doorway with his larger frame so Evangeline could not see who it was.

"Miss Genie, dinner is to be served momentarily." It was Fran, who she saw when looking around Camren. The maid met her gaze and smiled. "Perhaps a little fresh air will bring the flush from your face down a bit." Fran slid a look to Camren and then to the French doors.

"Thank you, Fran," Evangeline said and accepted Camren's hand to stand. She hurried to the doors and opened them. "We will be there shortly."

The cool breezed fanned over her overheated face and she gazed up to Camren. "They will be glad to hear we've decided to move forward with the ceremony."

He nodded. "I do have something to ask of you."

"Yes?"

"As laird of Clan Maclean, I am expected to marry in the presence of my clanspeople. My mother will want to plan our wedding ceremony. I wish to bring you to Scotland as my betrothed. Keep the fact we are actually married from them."

From the lowering of her brows and the crease between them, he expected her to be upset. However, Evangeline understood his responsibilities were an important part of his life.

"Of course. I understand and would not like for our marriage to have any negative effects on your clan. I have many questions about it."

A bell rang and she knew it was her mother's way of telling them to join them for dinner.

They entered the dining room moments later to find Gideon and her father in an animated discussion about horse breeds.

Her mother looked to her with a questioning gaze and Evangeline smiled and nodded. There was evident relief when her mother's shoulders fell.

"We have an announcement," Camren said and lifted his wine glass. "Evangeline and I have decided to move forward with the wedding. We shall be husband and wife the day after tomorrow."

"Bravo," her father said, lifting his glass. "Welcome to the family Laird Maclean."

"Please call me Camren. As you say, we will be family."

"I am so very happy," her mother said, her eyes shining with un-shed tears. "Finally."

Everyone laughed and drank from their glass.

Evangeline's heart expanded when her parents exchanged looks. They were very much in love and she knew they wished the same for her. Hopefully, the strong physical attraction between her and Camren would expand to something meaningful and rich.

Of all the things she'd expected in her life, the last thing would have been to be marrying the most handsome man she'd ever known and to move away from London to a totally different country.

Evangeline let out a breath and took a second sip of wine.

CHAPTER ELEVEN

LIKE THE DAY before, this morning was beautiful. Birdsong wafted through her open bedroom window announcing the start of a new day. Evangeline stretched lazily, having lingered in bed longer than she normally would.

Lucille had long given up and gone downstairs to seek Martha's assistance in being allowed out.

This would be her last morning waking in this house. The day would hold many firsts and many lasts. She planned to cherish each moment and not be hurried or bullied by the likes of Lucille, her mother or Martha. Even Camren would not be permitted to change her plans for the day.

"Good morning, Evangeline." Her mother, still in her dressing gown, entered the room and went to the window. She opened it wide and pulled the curtains open. "I ordered a perfect morning and I'm glad to see it was delivered." She turned to her, smiling. "How do you feel this morning?"

Evangeline sat up and fluffed the pillows so she could recline on them. "I am well. Not nervous. Not yet, anyway. I plan to take full advantage and enjoy each moment today."

"That is a wonderful plan." Her mother lowered to the bed. "I think you will be happy. Camren seems to be a kind and reasonable man."

Although she didn't know him or have any way to find out more since he wasn't a Londoner, Evangeline could only go from what she'd experienced. "He is smart. I would venture to say he seems to be very fair. I am not sure about his temperament, but he does seem to have restraint."

There was a twinkle in her mother's eyes. "And quite handsome, as well."

Evangeline chuckled. "There is that."

"I will miss you terribly. Your father barely got any sleep as I made him promise over and over again that we'd travel to Scotland regularly."

"Of course. I will also ensure Camren agrees that I come here, as well. He alluded that we'd spend an entire season here yearly."

"Wonderful," her mother said with a wide smile. She stood and leaned forward to place a kiss on Evangeline's forehead. "I love you, sweet girl." It was a statement she'd often repeated for as long as Evangeline could remember.

Instantly, tears formed and she blinked them away. "I love you, Mum."

"Now, would you like breakfast brought here or will you join your father and me in a bit?"

"I will be down momentarily to share my morning tea with Martha. Then I will dress and meet you and father for breakfast as usual."

"Very well," her mother replied, already leaving the room.

IF MARTHA WAS surprised when she entered the kitchen, she didn't show it. Instead, she motioned to the tea kettle. "I made some wonderful chamomile with a sprinkle of lavender."

"Perfect," Evangeline replied and poured the steaming liquid into a large cup. "I am going to enjoy our last morning, Martha. So tell me, how can I convince you to give me some of my favorite recipes?"

The woman pushed a notebook toward her. The inexpensive, rough cover reminded Evangeline of Martha. Rough exterior but a heart of gold. "I am ahead of you, girlie. I wrote these down over the years so that on your wedding day, it would be my gift to you."

Evangeline gasped and held it to her chest. "Thank you. This will be like you coming with me." She pushed from the table and rushed to Martha and hugged her.

"Don't make such a fuss now. I doubt the Scottish cook will be able to make them as good. But it's something if she tries." Martha dabbed at her eyes with the corner of her crisp apron. "I will miss these mornings with you, Miss Genie."

"I will, too," Evangeline replied. "I doubt Mother would allow you to come with me."

"Nor would I want to leave London," Martha said with a frown. "You will come visit often and that will be enough. Your marrying and moving to your own home are long overdue."

The rest of the morning passed quickly. Much too soon, it was time to get dressed for the ceremony, which was to take place in the garden. However, she lingered just a bit longer and watched the flurry of activity that had overtaken her home.

Extra help had been hired to set up chairs and decorate, which Evangeline enjoyed watching from the parlor windows. The garden was transformed into a magical place.

Tables with pastel clothes dotted the garden. Low vases spilling over with flowers had been placed on the center of each.

Her mother and Fran rushed from one spot to another, ensuring all was done perfectly. On occasion, they would look to Evangeline, who smiled back to let them know everything was perfect.

Rose and her mother arrived early. Her friend looked beautiful in a green, off the shoulder gown. "Why are you down here?" Rose hurried to her. "Your wedding is in two hours, there isn't time for you to dawdle."

They went up the stairs where Bridget, the hairdresser, and Mrs. Marigold, the seamstress, sat drinking tea. They, too, peered out the window to all that was happening.

Upon their entering, the women stood.

"Miss Prescott, I was about to come see about you," the hairdresser said with a warm smile.

Evangeline neared and sat on the chair they'd set up in the center of the room facing a three-way mirror. "I apologize. It was so entertaining to see all the preparations."

"We, too, enjoyed all the goings-on," the seamstress said as she looked over the gown that hung from the wardrobe.

"Please, Bridget, I prefer a simple upsweep, nothing too elaborate. The ceremony is taking place in the garden, so I prefer not to be overdone."

The seamstress gawked at Evangeline. "Miss Prescott, the bride should always stand out and outshine them all. The gown calls for a beautiful hairstyle with complicated twists and curl falls."

Evangeline and the hairdresser exchanged knowing looks. "I will see to it that her hair is perfectly in sync with her gown. Don't fret, Mrs. Marigold."

Thankfully, Bridget had done her hair for many an occasion and never failed to do exactly what Evangeline not only wished for, but styles that suited her perfectly.

Once her hair was done, she allowed the women present to assist with the gown. It was a lovely cream creation of tulle that flowed gently from her waist out to form a tulip shape. At the back, there was a short tail, perfect for an outdoor wedding. The bodice was formfitting, the sleeves tight on her arms in a see-through floral lace. The gown had a scalloped neckline edged in ruffled satin.

When she turned to look at herself, Evangeline's eyes rounded.

Was it really her? The woman looking back was splendid. Her eyes were a deeper rich green than usual, her cheeks pink from excitement.

The cream-colored wedding dress fit her body perfectly, the color enhancing the peach tone of her skin.

"Oh, Evangeline," her mother said as she entered and neared. "You look beautiful."

"Camren Maclean will not be able to pull his eyes away," Rose added.

Mrs. Marigold lifted up the veil and the hairdresser held a delicate, small flower crown. "Mistress, you are just in time to help with her veil," Bridget said.

"Perfect," her mother exclaimed and motioned for Rose to come closer. "We must help her to lower to this stool so we can put the flowers and veil on her head.

The veil lay across her head, the ends draping down her back and the flowers went atop and pinned to not hinder the intricate hairstyle.

Evangeline studied her reflection. She'd prefer not to have to wear the silly flowers or veil, but it was traditional, so she let it go without mention.

"People have arrived," Rose announced from the window. "I am going to step out and see who all is here." She walked out to the balcony and peered down.

Rose smiled widely and turned to Evangeline. "He's down there. He looks splendid and a bit pale."

Her mother chuckled. "When he got here, I offered him brandy and he took it without hesitation. It seems the imposing Scot is a bit nervous."

"I can certainly relate," Evangeline chastised them. "You shouldn't make light of it. My stomach is in knots and, now that you mention it, I would love a bit of brandy myself."

She sipped the brandy, allowing the warm liquid to settle into her. Just as she let out a breath, there was a rap at the door.

"It's time," her mother announced, seeming to suddenly become anxious herself.

THE CEREMONY WAS flawless, from the vows exchanged to the harp music filling the air.

As Evangeline allowed Camren to guide her to the head table, conversations around them were as light as the air.

She met his gaze for a long moment. "As lovely as this all is, I must admit to wishing to be away from it."

His lips curved. "And alone with me?"

"As much as I look forward to getting to know you better, what I meant is that I am not used to being the center of attention."

"Beautiful women should always get all the attention. Brides are the reason everyone attends these things." Camren squeezed her hand.

Across the room, her aunt and Lord Monroe stood with another couple. Although without Prudence, they seemed to be enjoying themselves.

Her parents wandered through the garden, greeting the small number of guests.

Rose was nowhere to be found and Evangeline strained to search for her. "Where is Rose?" she asked Camren. He scanned the area.

"I presume at the same place as Gideon, who is also missing at the moment."

"Oh, my." Evangeline gave Camren and incredulous look. "Do you really think so?"

The rest of the festivities included cutting the cake, chatting with the guests and seeing off the clergyman. It seemed too soon when it was time for the newlyweds to be sent off themselves.

Evangeline had changed into a lighter pale blue gown and, along with Camren, they climbed into his carriage to head to his townhouse. Camren informed her that Gideon would be staying at his newly acquired home until they returned to Scotland.

"Are you bringing a maid with you?" Camren asked, looking out of the window.

"Here she comes." Evangeline motioned to a frazzled Fran, who was assisted onto the bench next to Camren's driver.

Evangeline wanted to giggle at the way Fran waved at the group gathered as if it were she who was being seen off. Camren didn't seem to notice anything, until she nudged him. "Wave."

They both did and, finally, rode away from the wedding ceremony and the home she'd lived in her entire life. As excited as Evangeline was at the prospect of a new start, she couldn't help the tang of sadness the moment brought.

"Other than your maid and my steward, we will be alone this evening. I wanted to ensure it would be comfortable and not over-whelming for you."

Evangeline nodded and let out a breath. "Thank you."

"The housekeeper and the chambermaid will return in the morning. So there is no need to fret over breakfast."

Was he rambling? Evangeline slid a look to him, and he took her hand and squeezed it. "If you wish to wait for us to... be together, I understand. Our marriage is not traditional, so I am willing to take things at your pace."

She leaned into him and put her head on his shoulder. "Thank you. It means a great deal to me to hear you say that. How do you feel?"

A deep chuckle rumbled in his chest. "I want to be with you and make you my wife fully as is customary. To have a wedding night. At the same time, I know we do not know each other well."

"I want to start our marriage being honest. I appreciate your candor. I will spend our first night in your bed as your wife."

He squeezed her hand and nodded.

The carriage came to a stop and the driver opened the door. Fran stood by the side as Evangeline emerged, assisted by Camren.

The townhouse was dim with just enough light for them to make their way inside and up the stairs.

A woman fetched Fran and they disappeared, leaving Evangeline and Camren alone.

"This way," he said as he took Evangeline's elbow and they climbed up the staircase. The thuds of her heart echoed in her ears.

He opened the door and led her into his bedroom. The room had obviously been cleaned recently, the bed perfectly made. Although the room was definitely masculine with no frills, it was nicely decorated.

"Can I help you undress?" Camren came close to her, his gaze on her. "Or would you like to summon the maid?"

"I can manage." Evangeline placed a flattened hand on his chest. "Do you require assistance?" Her lips curved when he frowned.

"No."

"Good," she replied, lifting to her toes and pressing a kiss to his jaw. "I don't wish to help you, but instead watch as you undress."

His chest expanded at her words and he turned his head and pressed his lips to hers. The kiss was tentative, seeking acceptance.

Evangeline wanted to prolong their first time, so she moved her mouth to the side of his and pressed her lips there.

"Toying with me?" Camren teased. "What is this game we play?"

She didn't respond, but instead turned away. "On second thought, I do require help with the buttons."

Chilled air caressed her exposed skin as each inch of fabric fell away. Camren's warm mouth trailed down her back, teasing, nipping and licking a path.

Arching and allowing her head to fall back, Evangeline could not contain the soft moan that escaped or the shivers of anticipation flooding her senses.

Just as he reached the last button, she stepped away and turned. "I can continue on my own. Thank you."

The darkening of his eyes gave him a feral look and she knew not to toy overmuch with him. Moving closer to the bed, he stood with hands to the sides.

Evangeline allowed her gaze to travel over his body. He was quite devastatingly attractive.

Heart thundering, she lowered the top of her dress, pushed it past her hips and let it fall to the soft carpet. Next, she bent at the waist and removed her shoes. It was more a ploy to give him a clear view down the front of her chemise as it would have been easy to kick them off.

When she straightened, instead of removing her chemise, she pulled pins from her hair, allowing the tresses to fall about her shoulders.

His gaze never left her as he removed his boots and cravat. Each movement was precise, making her wonder if that would be how he made love.

Although he unbuttoned the front of his breeches, he didn't remove them. A delightful tease, Evangeline considered following the light feathering of hair from the center of his stomach to the hidden place.

He closed the distance between them. "I cannot wait. Remove your clothes, vixen." Closing his mouth over hers, Evangeline lost control and ran her hands down the wide expanse of his back. He was warm and strong, each inch wonderfully smooth under her hands.

When her palm slid over a scar, she decided it would be something she'd have to ask about later because, in that moment, he lifted her up and carried her to stand beside the bed.

"Too many clothes," Camren muttered, pushing her chemise down her shoulders, the light garment easily falling to her hips.

She pushed it down and, upon straightening, stopped to gawk as he pushed his pants down.

Before she could take him all in, once again she found herself in his arms. Evangeline wanted to protest, to see all of him, but at the first touch of skin against skin, she lost her ability to speak.

His hands roamed over her body as his tongue delved past parted lips. They remained standing, exploring one another with hands, fingers and lips.

"I want you so much," Evangeline said and gasped when he lifted her again, this time lowering her to the bed as he climbed in along with her.

His body was instantly over hers, the weight perfect as she fought to keep her eyes open and take in his darkened eyes. "You are so very beautiful. Perfect in every way."

Camren hungered for her and didn't care about her past nor did he seem particularly bothered by her leg.

Lifting up to place weight on his thighs, Camren took to her breasts, holding them with both hands, suckling at one and then the other.

Sensations that had been buried for so long surfaced, molten hot trails blazing paths to her core and down both legs.

Struggling to keep from losing herself completely, she lifted her hips to him, asking without words for their bodies to join.

Camren met her gaze for a moment and smiled down at her.

At first, the nudge was gentle, his hard member seeking entrance. Camren pushed into her and hesitated. Although her body expanded to accept him, Evangeline stiffened, a bit fearful as he was much larger than Avery.

Unsure of what to expect, she let out a long breath as he pushed in with one strong, fluid thrust.

Evangeline gasped at the fullness, her body relaxing around him. It was absolutely marvelous how wonderfully they fit together.

Within moments, he was driving in and out, a steady rhythm so utterly perfect that tears filled her eyes.

"Oh-oh-oh," Evangeline repeated and cupped his bottom with both hands, urging him to drive deeper.

His deep, happy grunts intermingled with her higher exclamations as they continued to move, the pace faster as they inched toward culmination. Evangeline lost the fight first, cresting and falling, her body shuddering with release.

In a fog, Camren's moan permeated and he thrust deep twice before spilling.

Rolling to his back, he pulled her against his side and kissed her temple.

"Ummggghhh." His incoherent mumblings were cute and Evangeline smiled.

She pressed a soft kiss to his jaw. "I agree."

They fell into an exhausted slumber until the middle of the night when, upon sensing someone beside her, Evangeline was startled awake.

The soft snoring, although a bit jarring, announced her new life and the man she'd be sharing a bed with for the rest of her life.

Her lips curved when he smacked his lips and rolled to his back. She couldn't make out his features in the dark, but his moonlit profile was as perfect as he was.

Evangeline snuggled against her husband and, within minutes, fell back asleep.

Sometime later, she woke when an arm snaked around her waist, pulling her against him.

CHAPTER TWELVE

C AMREN OPENED HIS eyes and blinked as sunlight hit his face. Normally an early riser, it was rare that his room would be so bright when waking. He turned slowly to his new bride. Fast asleep, her hair askew and pink lips slightly parted, she was enticing.

Admittedly, he'd fantasized about waking up to her and what she'd look like unencumbered by hair pins or clothes. In reality, she was more breathtaking than any of his fantasies.

The rumpled blankets surrounded her like a nest, and he leaned closer, enjoying the sight of her pert breasts.

She took a deep breath and released it slowly and shifted, continuing to sleep. Camren placed his lips at the top of her right breast allowing his mouth to linger on the satiny skin. Already, his erection was so hard it was almost painful.

"Mm mm," Evangeline's eyelids lifted slowly, and her lips curved. "Yes." Her soft whisper gave the permission he needed to sink himself into her and live out the fantasy of waking up to a beautiful, sensual siren.

They made love lazily until the need for completion sent the pace to quicken.

Evangeline lay sprawled over his chest as he traced circles on her soft skin.

"We should get up," Camren said. "I smelled breakfast quite a while ago. Flora, the housekeeper, is here."

Evangeline peered up at him and again he wanted to make love to her. "I am very hungry."

He admired the view of her slipping from the bed and walking across the room. Her body was delightful. Pert, full breasts, a small waist and ample hips.

She pulled a robe on and gave him a flirty smile. "You have no idea how alluring you look, laying there watching me."

He crooked a finger. "Come here."

"No. If we don't get dressed now, we will miss breakfast," Evangeline replied and hurried behind a screen in the corner of the room.

DURING BREAKFAST, EACH time their gazes met, a flush of heat traveled through Evangeline's body. Her mind scrambled to grasp that the handsome man on the other side of the table from her was, indeed, her husband.

Unlike her, he seemed nonplussed, giving his valet, Daniel, instructions on what to do that day. He had business to attend to which, in Evangeline's estimation, could have been left off for at least a day.

She tapped her finger on the table and both men turned to her. "What am I to do here alone all day if you plan to attend to business?"

The men exchanged confused glances.

"Perhaps visit with your friend?" Gideon had arrived and provided an answer, making the other men in the room let out relieved breaths.

Evangeline pinned Gideon with a glare. "Thank you for pointing out something my poor, feeble mind could not conjure. What I am attempting to point out is that your friend here..." she motioned to Camren, "... and I got married yesterday. It is customary for newly-weds to spend time and get to know each other for... oh, I don't know… at least several days."

The room went silent. A maid who stood at the door giggled and quickly raced away.

"Yes," Camren replied. "You are correct, dear. Other than a quick dash to the docks to meet about business, I do plan to spend the rest of the day here."

When she lifted an eyebrow, Gideon cleared his throat. "Or I could go."

"Or Gideon can go." By the crinkle between his brows, Camren did not like the new plan.

Evangeline stood and rolled her eyes. "I am going to visit my mother for the rest of the morning. Carry on and do as you wish. I would prefer the company of someone who wishes mine."

At entering the bedroom, she stifled a chuckle. Men were such strange creatures.

Camren entered and came up behind her. "I apologize. We can spend the day together. Go for a ride to Hyde Park. I do wish to spend time with you. It was thoughtless of me to not consider that I was leaving you alone the day after marrying." Camren wrapped his arms around her waist and nuzzled her hair. "Forgive me."

Evangeline turned in his arms and looked into his eyes. "If you must conduct business today, then do it. Your mind will be elsewhere if you do not."

After a soft kiss, he shook his head. "No, we shall postpone business for a few days. Gideon is going to meet with the man I planned to see. I will follow up in a few days."

A PAINFUL TWINGE woke Evangeline early one morning. She winced as her injured leg cramped. The room was cool as the fire in the hearth had waned, so she snuggled deeper into the blankets.

Camren stood beside the wardrobe. He was shirtless and seemed at a loss as to what to wear.

They'd been married just seven days and, already, Evangeline was accustomed to his daily presence. His muscles bunched and smoothed as he pulled on a shirt he'd chosen, and she was disappointed when his smooth skin was covered.

"What is that scar on your back from?"

He turned to her with a slight frown. "Sword fight. I was young and should have known better than to turn my back."

"How barbaric. Why were you in a fight with swords?" Her eyes rounded as she imagined him fighting, warrior against warrior, atop a horse.

"It was a competition. We have Highland games that take place yearly, I often compete.

She studied him for a moment. "Only men would consider something that could kill you a game."

"True," he said with a grin. "It makes one's blood rush, which is enjoyable."

Nearing the bed, he leaned forward. "I have a business meeting and will be back in a few hours." When his mouth took hers, she reached for his neck and pulled him closer.

"Don't tarry."

"I most definitely will not." His gaze moved to where the blankets had slipped, exposing her breasts. "I cannot fathom the thought of leaving you neglected in any form."

Evangeline pulled up the bedding and shook her head. "Be with care."

WHEN SHE SAT at the breakfast table minutes later, the housekeeper entered and brought her eggs and toast.

"How are you today, Flora?" Evangeline asked the older woman.

"Very well, indeed, My Lady."

Since the first time it was used, the title gave Evangeline pause. For some reason, she'd not given thought to the fact she was marrying a titled man. "I am glad to hear that, Flora. Can I ask, have there ever been any dogs or cats here?"

"Only horses," Flora said with a smile.

"I am considering whether or not to bring my cat, Lucille, here. You see, my cat is quite attached to me. However," Evangeline hesitated. "That cat is set in its ways."

The woman nodded. "Cats are adept at adjusting to their surroundings. I have two myself."

Evangeline smiled widely. "I knew there was something endearing about you."

The woman chuckled.

"I think I will go visit my mother today and get her thoughts on it. Would you happen to know Martha Downy?"

"I do, My Lady," Flora said. "She is a friend of mine. We see each other at the market. She has asked about you and told me you are a very nice person."

Her chest tightened. Other than her parents, she missed Martha so very much. Fran had been sick for the last few days, so she'd had little interaction with anyone familiar.

"How is Fran?"

"About the same, she is lingering. It is best you remain away from her as whatever ails her could be contagious. Her mother came and is caring for her in the cottage house."

It had been generous of Camren to allow Fran and her mother to remain there while Fran recovered. The young woman had been a bit sickly of late, which made Evangeline worry about taking her to Scotland.

"What, exactly, do you suppose is wrong with her?" she asked

Flora.

The housekeeper shook her head. "The doctor said her lungs were not filling with air properly."

Upon arriving at her parents' home, Evangeline hesitated at the front door. It felt strange that it was not her home any longer.

"Good morning, darling." Her mother appeared and hugged her tightly. "How are you?"

"I am well. Very worried about Fran. She is not getting better."

Her mother sighed. "We have been praying for her. Martha is quite upset about it, as well. You will have to hire someone to look after your needs until Fran gets better."

"That is precisely what I came to speak to you about. How to go about hiring someone. I hate that Fran will probably not go to Scotland with me. She was so looking forward to it, but I'm afraid it's best for her to remain."

They entered the kitchen and Martha greeted her by motioning to the doorway. "Lucille just went out again. I think your cat is searching for you, Miss Genie. Poor thing."

No sooner did the woman finish the sentence then Lucille appeared and pranced to Evangeline. The cat rubbed against her legs, purring with glee.

"I think Lucille should come with me. I miss this cat terribly," Evangeline announced.

"What about Camren?" her mother asked. "I am not sure he will take well to a cat sleeping in your bed. That cat is very spoiled. It will be hard to keep Lucille away."

Evangeline lifted the cat up and kissed the furry face. "We will have to work on a new sleeping arrangement for you, Miss Lucille."

They drank tea and discussed finding a new maid with Martha who had her fingers on the pulse of what was happening around town. Many times, young women seeking employment would ask others at the market about any availability.

"Since Lord Singletary died, the entire staff was relieved of their positions. There are plenty looking for a position such as this. They come from a well-established home and will be trustworthy."

"Will you seek someone for me please, Martha?" Evangeline asked. "I trust your judgment. You know me better than I know myself sometimes."

She visited for another hour, mostly because she didn't relish the idea of returning to the empty house even if only a few miles away.

"You should find things to do. Embroidery, reading, maybe start gardening," her mother suggested. "I know it's a time of adjustment, but with Camren having a tight schedule before returning to Scotland, it is understandable that he has to be away from home most days."

"I am not complaining," Evangeline said. "That is why I wish to bring Lucille and also I will train a new maid and that will occupy my time."

They went out the front door together to the family carriage. It would take her back to the townhouse and Evangeline hugged her mother. "Please tell Martha to hurry. The chambermaid tries her best, but she had no idea how to style my hair. I am glad to only be coming here."

After a hug and picking up a carrier with a very angry Lucille in it, Evangeline climbed into the carriage and headed back home.

Along the way, there were noticeably many people out enjoying the warm weather. Evangeline had not considered a day of shopping.

Upon arriving home, she'd make a long list of things to acquire before her move to Scotland. Rose would enjoy helping her acquire what would be needed.

Her lips curved at plans that would keep her occupied for a few days at least.

The house was quiet, and she spent a long while following Lucille about as the cat familiarized itself with the house. By late afternoon, the feline had claimed a chaise near a large window and slept soundly in the sun.

Evangeline sat at a drawing table and penned a list of things to purchase. Although she wasn't sure about the common spaces at the keep in Scotland and knowing she'd not have any control over décor or such, Camren had told her their chambers included a sitting room and dressing room, as well.

She'd ensure there was a writing desk as she'd make use of it to maintain communications with her mother and Rose. Since the area where the Maclean home was located sounded rural, she would purchase papers, books and plenty of her favorite chocolates.

The list was becoming quite long. She and Rose would be occupied for days completing the task.

"Would you like dinner served now, Lady Maclean?" Flora asked while lighting lanterns around the room. "It is quite late."

Evangeline frowned, doing her best to remember what Camren had said before leaving that morning. "Laird Maclean should have returned by now. Can you send a message to Mister Sutherland and find out if he is there?"

"Of course, Lady Maclean." With a worried look directed at her, the woman hurried away.

Something seemed odd about Camren's absence. Daniel was not there either, so she couldn't inquire about his whereabouts.

CHAPTER THIRTEEN

S WAYING MOVEMENT BROUGHT Camren out of a strange sleep of sorts. He blinked and swallowed past his parched throat.

The surroundings were dim and stunk of rotted fish. A boat, a small vessel if he were to guess, was where he found himself.

His mind flashed to having come to the docks to meet a captain of a ship that was to bring whisky for his and Gideon's company to England. He'd not found the man and, while waiting, had been overtaken by four or five rather rough-looking men.

Beefy fists had pummeled him until he'd fallen to the ground. The only good thing was that he'd managed to knock a few teeth out of a couple of their mouths.

"What in the bloody hell?" He struggled to stand, swaying from being unconscious and pain assailing him. He had no shoes and his jacket was gone. When he breathed in, Camren flinched. His ribs hurt. Probably had several broken ones.

They'd not bothered to tie him up, which was idiotic. Then again, it was evident the goons had been sent to beat him and get rid of him immediately.

At the sounds of footsteps, he dropped to the ground and pretended to be passed out.

"How you plan to get rid of 'im?" a gruff voice asked.

"Toss 'im overboard. The man's out cold and will drown," a second answered.

There were chuckles.

"We got what we wanted from the man. It seems cruel to let 'im die." Camren held his breath, waiting for the others to reply. With broken ribs, it would be quite hard to swim. Not only that, he had no idea how far out they'd gone.

They grabbed his hands and feet and Camren bit back a cry at the pain the movements caused.

As the men struggled to stay upright, he assessed pain in his ribs, his left hip and face.

Peering from under his eyelids, he caught sight of how far shore was. He could barely make it out. By the pains shooting from his sides, he hadn't the strength to fight and resisting would only bring more injuries that he could ill afford.

Going limp made the men stumble as his weight became uneven.

"I think 'e passed out again," one of them said.

"Hopefully, 'e'll die quickly. Poor bastard."

Just as they swung him to toss him overboard, Camren took a deep swallow of air. But at the shock of the cold water, it was forced from him. For a moment, he let his body adjust and then painfully arched his back and floated up.

He'd have to be careful to ensure not to be seen. So despite the desperate need for air, he waited a bit just under the surface.

When his lungs began to burn, screaming for air, he carefully surfaced but just enough to gulp in air.

He waited a bit more and then came up fully for air, coughing and choking. He turned in every direction as he looked for the boat. Whatever way they went had to be toward shore. He finally caught a glimpse of it. He was weak, cold and in pain. How far could he swim before succumbing?

A SLEEPY DANIEL opened the door when Evangeline pounded for the fourth or fifth time. His eyes widened. "Lady Maclean..." he peered around her. "Is something amiss?"

"You could say that. It is late morning and I have not seen my husband since yesterday morning. He said he was going to the docks, but never returned."

She tapped her foot impatiently. "May I come in?"

"Oh, yes... of course. I do apologize."

By the smell of his breath, he and whoever was there had done a lot of drinking. She stopped in the entry and remained standing since there were no furnishings. "Is he here?"

"I will search immediately. However, Mister Gideon and I went to bed quite late and he was not here then."

A shirtless Gideon appeared at the top of the stairs. "What is going on?"

"It seems Laird Maclean is missing."

"I will get our horses immediately." As if someone pushed him from behind, Gideon raced down the stairs, grabbed a shirt from the banister, tossed it on and ran past her. He reappeared moments later wearing a coat and boots. His gaze moved to her.

"Please contact the constable. Tell him and his men to meet me at the docks. I will come to the townhouse to let you know of any news." Without another word, he raced out. She guessed to find his horse.

"We will find him." Daniel was a bit slower. But he, too, appeared dressed and hurried out after giving her a curt bow.

It wasn't until she stood in the empty house alone that Evangeline's chest tightened. Where was her husband?

She turned to the waiting cabby in a daze. "To the constable's office please."

Two hours later, she paced the parlor at the townhouse while her mother and Rose sat in silence.

"Why hasn't someone come to bring news yet?" Evangeline said with exasperation. "I am of half a mind to go to the docks myself."

"That is no place for a woman. There are too many ruffians and undesirables there," Rose said, sounding more like her mother.

Her mother patted the seat next to her. "Sit for a moment, dear. We can only get in the way if we go down there. I am sure Gideon and the constable have things well in hand."

"I waited too long," Evangeline said, sinking down to sit. "What if he was killed? I should have checked on him before going to bed."

"I would have probably done the same," Rose said. "You don't know Camren well enough to ascertain what is normal or not in his habits."

Her mother patted her hand. "We should pray for his safety."

Three bangs on the door made them all jump. A maid hurried past and, moments later, a young man in uniform entered.

"Lady Maclean?" He identified himself as a policeman, his face solemn. "We found someone who witnessed your husband being assaulted by three men. He was taken out on a boat. We have several out now searching the water in case he was tossed."

Evangeline's breath caught. His words seemed to float over her. Was she to become a widow just a week after marrying? How was it possible?

"Did no one try to help him?" Rose asked, her face pinched with worry.

The man shook his head. "These are everyday occurrences there, unfortunately."

Evangeline jumped to her feet. "So, the answer is no. People stood by while my husband was beaten by a group of men. How can this be? Aren't your people assigned there to keep watch?"

"There are several, yes, but we cannot see everything." The man took a step back, as if expecting to become a victim of a beating himself.

Her mother came to her side. "Thank you for informing us. Do they know how long it's been since he was taken out on the boat?"

"This morning, Ma'am. Perhaps two or three hours ago."

The man was shown out by Rose.

When Evangeline closed her eyes, the tears trickled from the corners of her eyes. "He cannot possibly survive that long out there. What will happen, Mother? What about his family?"

"Let's not think the worst, darling." By the tremble in her mother's voice, she, too, was expecting that news would not be good.

THROUGHOUT THE REST of the day, men stopped by to give reports. Camren had not been found. Both Gideon and Daniel were on two different boats, refusing to give up searching. However, as the morning turned to afternoon and then to evening, hope of finding Camren alive diminished each hour that passed.

Finally, when it became too dark to continue searching, Daniel return. He looked haggard and refused to look Evangeline in the eyes.

"I should have gone with him," he said, sinking into a chair near the hearth.

No one said anything.

Both Evangeline's mother and Rose continued to sit with her. Moments later, her father appeared. Evangeline was shocked to see he looked as tired as Daniel.

"Are you unwell?" Evangeline asked.

"No," her father shook his head. "I've been out looking for Camren and have failed to find him."

Everyone remained in the parlor, Rose and her mother dozing

with blankets tucked around them. No one wanted to leave the room in case news came. Evangeline went up to her room to retrieve a shawl. Upon spotting the last shirt Camren wore, she lifted it and smelled it.

She didn't even realize her knees had given out and that sobs racked her body until someone came and hugged her.

"I know, darling, I know." Rose tightened her hold and they cried together.

CHAPTER FOURTEEN

"E VANGELINE." THE DEEP voice roused her from a fitful slumber, and she looked up to see Gideon stood over her.

It was early morning, the sun barely filtering through the window. Pale with dark purpling under his eyes, the man looked about to pass out from exhaustion.

"Yes?" Evangeline straightened and immediately was wide awake. Rose, who'd fallen asleep with her on a chaise in the parlor, also sat up.

Gideon smiled. "We found him."

Her heart thundered and she gasped, not quite sure she wanted to hear the rest. "Where is he?"

"At the hospital. Camren is alive."

Once again, her knees threatened to give out, but Evangeline refused to fall. "I must go right away. Let me just freshen up." She hurried from the room, rushing up to the bedroom.

There were voices and lots of talking as the others rose and were now peppering Gideon with questions. Evangeline had heard the three words she'd been praying for. Camren was alive.

On the carriage ride to the hospital, Gideon met her gaze. "You have to be prepared. He was beaten and has broken ribs. It was a miracle that he survived for as long as he did in the water. Thankfully, a fisherman spotted and rescued him from certain death."

"We will find the man and pay him handsomely," her father stated. They were crowded into the carriage, but no one wanted to be away from each other. Rose, Evangeline and her mother were on one seat. Across from them were Gideon and her father. Daniel drove the carriage at a fast pace through the early morning, almost empty London streets.

Upon arriving, they were quickly guided to a private room where the nurse hesitated and met Evangeline's gaze. "You may bring one other person with you."

Evangeline took her mother's hand. "My mother will come inside with me."

They walked in silently, the only sounds those of people in the hallway outside.

The bed upon which Camren lay was slim. He filled it both width and length. His face was a swollen, both eyes with dark bruising, and his bottom lip was cut. There was a long cut on the left side of his face that had been stitched.

"Oh, goodness," her mother whispered. "The poor man."

Both of his hands were wrapped with white cloth, probably because his knuckles were cut and battered.

"He's sleeping right now because we gave him a sedative. It's best he rests to allow his body to recover. Other than the visible bruising, he has several broken ribs and a cut just above the hairline... here." She pointed to right side of his head. The area has been shaved and stitched. Evangeline leaned over him to inspect the area, but she could not see because of the bandages.

"Has he been awake and spoken?"

The nurse nodded. "Yes, he was conscious when they brought him in, but he was a bit confused."

After a stern warning not to wake him, the nurse walked out.

Evangeline turned to see all the faces outside the door and then to her mother. "Gideon and Daniel should be able to come in. After they leave to get some rest, I will remain here with him. Why don't you and Father take Rose home and sleep for a bit?"

Her mother looked to Camren for a long moment. "I will return early this afternoon and take you to have something to eat."

Evangeline nodded, just then remembering she'd not eaten anything since the morning before. Even though Flora had cooked dinner, she'd been too worried to eat, her stomach in knots. The food had little appeal.

"Thank you," she said, accepting a hug from her mother.

"He is a strong man and therefore I am sure he will recover fully," her mother assured her.

Gideon and Daniel entered the room when she and her mother emerged. Rose hugged her, also promising to return once she changed clothing. When her father's strong arms held her for a bit longer than necessary, Evangeline sagged. "I don't know what I'd do without you and Mum," she murmured against his chest.

Her father patted her back. "We'll always be here for you."

"I will stay here with Evangeline. Both of you should go get rest," Gideon told those present.

Daniel scowled. "I prefer to go to the docks and do some investigating."

"Please don't go there. The same men are probably still there and could hurt you, as well," Evangeline told him.

Daniel pressed his lips together. "Very well. I will go speak to the constable then and find out if anyone has been detained." He stormed from the room, leaving Evangeline with Gideon.

"Who was he supposed to meet?"

"A shipper we are hiring to transport the whisky from Scotland to London. The man is well known and trustworthy. He did not show up for the meeting because a message was delivered to him putting the meeting off for another day. Although he was at the docks when Camren was attacked, he was too far from where it happened to see anything."

Evangeline straightened. "So, the attack was planned then? Who would do something like that?"

"We have competition. Someone who is afraid we will dent their profits. I have an idea of who and I'm hoping once Camren comes to, he will confirm my suspicions. They are not aware Camren is still alive. The constable has agreed to keep it a secret in hopes that those responsible will return to the docks."

It was late in the day when Camren's eyes finally opened. He looked around the room and then to her for a moment and then looked away. Evangeline squeezed his hand.

A light flush colored his face and she wondered if he was embarrassed to have been bested and so badly beaten. He was, after all, a good-sized man, masculine and trained to fight.

"Look at me, Camren," she told him in a stern voice and waited until he did. Her chest constricted when he let out a long sigh and winced. Finally, he met her gaze again. There was an angry, red stain in his right eye, probably when he was kicked in the face.

"It is incredible that you survived. A testament to your will to live, strength and bravery."

"I don't feel brave right now. Or particularly in good shape." He shrugged. "The cold water helped, I think."

"Yes, that is precisely what the doctor said. That in a way, being thrown into the water saved your life."

"I thought about you and how my dying would affect your future." Scanning her face, he frowned. "You look tired. Go home and get some rest."

Evangeline shook her head. "I want to be here. I'd only worry if I went home. If you had not returned, I would have been devasted. Those hours, when we didn't know where you were, had to be the most horrible of my life. I've come to care for you a great deal, Husband, and do not wish to return to life before meeting you."

"Thinking that I didn't wish for you to be with anyone else propelled me to fight to stay alive. I'm a selfish bastard."

She chuckled and pressed a hand to his shoulder. "How valiant of you, Laird Maclean."

They discussed the logistics of his recovery and decided to postpone their return to Scotland for another month until he could travel without issue. Finally, Daniel and Gideon arrived and, with much prodding from the men, she was driven home to spend the night.

The next day, Camren would be sent home to recover and she had to ensure a downstairs bedroom was prepared.

CHAPTER FIFTEEN

CAMREN FOUGHT AGAINST a wave of nausea from the sedatives. When a nurse attempted to give him more, he refused it. "I will not have a problem sleeping this night," he informed her.

Once the woman left, his attention went back to Gideon and Daniel. "Yes, as you probably suspect, it was O'Hara, who had me attacked. I heard one of the men mention his name. The bastard is trying to keep us from expanding our business here. The men who beat me were Irish."

"I will personally hunt him down and teach him a lesson." Daniel crossed his arms and glared.

"There is little we can do without rousing the local authorities' suspicions," Gideon said, shaking his head. "He won't remain in London. He has probably already returned to the sea." He gave Camren a pointed look. "When your brother finds out about this, he will not hesitate to ensure O'Hara never sails again."

Not one to condone violence, Camren would have normally rebuffed the idea. This time, however, considering O'Hara meant for him to be killed, he wouldn't stop his brother from ensuring the man didn't hurt anyone else.

His younger brother, Cowan, was hot-tempered and the ruin of many a seaworthy vessel, especially if it compromised his privateering pursuits.

Rarely did Cowan go near England because he'd be arrested on sight. Currently, he was probably somewhere near Scotland. His brother did well for himself sailing between the Caribbean and Scotland, often paid to transport goods for wealthy investors.

"Send Cowan a message. Ensure he knows to spare as many lives as he can."

Gideon laughed. "He will receive the message, see red and then do as he pleases, you know that."

It was true, his brother was fiercely protective of the family. "Should we handle it differently then?"

When his friend gave him a two-shouldered shrug, Camren knew it was too late. The message had been sent prior to him coming to.

"GOOD MORNING." EVANGELINE pressed a kiss to Camren's jaw, and he turned to her, with only a slight twinge of pain. Finally, he'd been able to join her in bed after sleeping in a downstairs bedroom recuperating for three weeks.

Although they'd made love the night before, it hadn't been his best performance. His wife had proven to be creative in a way that had ensured he'd been more than pleasured, but he was sure she'd not been as much.

"I promise to make it up to you," he said and pressed his lips to her throat. The fast pulse was a telltale sign she enjoyed his hands traveling over her body.

Pushing his hands away, she slid out of bed. "Don't start that again. We have much to do. Today, my things will be crated and shipped to Scotland. I have much to do before they come this morning."

He lifted to his elbows and watched as she scrambled into a dressing gown. Then she opened the door to her ill-tempered cat who'd been scratching at it for the last half-hour.

The feline entered and looked to them with narrowed eyes before digging its claws into the carpet and stretching.

"Lucille, you may as well get used to constant change." Evangeline bent at the waist and patted the cat's head. "We are moving once again." She turned to Camren. "I've never asked. Do you have a pet?"

"I have a hunting dog. His name is Hound."

"Surely you jest?" His wife gave him an incredible look. "Hound? Why would you not name your dog?"

"I named him Hound after my brother, Ian, named his Dog."

She shook her head and sighed. "I certainly hope your hound is not unfriendly toward Lucille."

"I have no idea. There is a cat in the kitchen and, as far as I know, Hound spends time there and has not attacked the overweight animal."

"Good." She went to the wardrobe and inspected her clothes. In the mornings, watching his wife dress had become a favorite pastime of his. Soon, however, things would change dramatically. He would once again regain the helm and run the clan. Duties would include overseeing court in the mornings, visiting the villages and farms in the afternoons and hosting visitors many evenings.

There was little time to rest and sleep for him back home. But now that he'd discovered how nice it was, he vowed to relax his schedule some.

Evangeline's new maid, Molly, walked in and helped with the fastening of the gown she chose. Then after his wife sat, the maid styled her hair. Once that was complete, Evangeline poured tea for both of them and brought his to the bed.

"You are becoming quite spoiled, Laird Maclean." She put the cup and saucer on the side table. She waited for him to sit up against the pillows and then pushed the cup into his hands. "Is this how I should expect our marriage will continue?" she teased.

The liquid was perfectly soothing as it entered his body.

"Unfortunately, no. Which is something I must warn you about. There are many duties that I must oversee once we return to my home. You, as well. My mother will ensure you are informed and if you need any assistance, I am certain she will see to any need."

"I doubt the customs of running a home are very different than here. I am sure I can adjust."

He wanted to reassure her, but the differences were vast. "People dress more, how should I say it, serviceable. My mother and sister work in the gardens to ensure there is enough produce for the clan's people. Most meals are attended by at least twenty."

"Oh." She sank onto the bed. "Please tell me more."

"There are many differences between life in rural Scotland and here. I don't wish to scare you but, there, my family is self-reliant when it comes to making many things that are more easily available for purchase in the city. However, you are correct. I imagine it's not much different than life in the countryside here."

Men's voices downstairs alerted them to visitors.

"I look forward to the change," Evangeline said with a firm nod and stood. "I'd better go see who is here. It may be the men here to pack things up."

"I will join you shortly," Camren said and emptied his tea.

CHAPTER SIXTEEN

EXHAUSTION DID NOT take away Evangeline's appreciation for the stunning scenery as they neared Fort William where Camren's home was.

The weather had become measurably cooler and from what she could see, the few people that were out and about dressed more for suitability to the surroundings than for fashion. Since traveling through Scotland, she'd yet to see a pretty gown or any sort of shops like those in London.

Camren slept next to her in the carriage. He'd ridden on his horse part of the way, as Gideon and Daniel did now, but was not yet recovered enough to continue for as long.

There were raps at the top of the carriage and Camren straightened. "We must be arriving."

She leaned out to look and lost her ability to breath at the view before her. A stone castle stood proud with mountains as a backdrop. There was a wide road leading up to it. On the roadside, people milled about, some with baskets filled with items, others urging sheep to move forward.

"There certainly are a lot of people about," Evangeline said. "Your home is immense."

Following her line of sight, he motioned to the left. "The larger part of Clan Maclean is located off the coast on the Isle of Mull. My clan is smaller here, but we do a lot of travel back and forth with my father's family."

"Smaller?" She couldn't imagine how huge that place would be if the building before them was the smaller of the two. "Exactly how many people live here?"

He looked at the building and his lips curved. "My mother, brothers, Ian's wife, my uncle, his wife and my three cousins. The head of the guard, Gideon, Daniel and six guardsmen. There are more men who live in guard quarters on the west side. The stable master, his two lads, then there are the servants, I believe there are twelve of them, the gardener, they all live in cottages to the east. The housekeeper and her husband..."

"Never mind," Evangeline said in an awed whisper at they entered a huge courtyard. At the entrance, which was arched with immense wooden doors, stood a group of people. One of the men had a remarkable likening to Camren, so she knew it had to be one of his brothers. Two women, one older and one younger, also looked alike in coloring to Camren. It had to be his mother and sister. Evangeline attempted to recall their names, but her brain could barely function at the realization of how utterly different her life was about to be.

They pulled to a stop and, immediately, Camren climbed down. He was hugged by the women and his brother at the same time. None of them hesitating to show their happiness at his return.

Evangeline smiled at the warmth of his family. She was glad to know they were a caring group of people. However, moments later, her thinking came to a halt when a woman sauntered up to her husband and pulled him into a tight hug. She then held his face in her hands and spoke to him.

For a moment, Evangeline wondered if he'd forgotten about her, especially when Gideon and Daniel dismounted and were also received warmly.

When the older woman turned to the carriage and saw her, she hurried over with hands extended. "Poor child, we have not properly greeted you." She looked to Camren who walked up behind. "You left her in here. She must think we have the worst manners."

"Not at all," Evangeline said as she was helped from the carriage and Camren pulled her hand to the crook of his arm. Evangeline couldn't help but slide a look to the woman who'd hugged him earlier. Sure enough, she'd turned a bright shade of red and glared back.

"Mother, this is my betrothed, Evangeline Prescott."

"Please call me Mariel," the woman said and hugged her. "Welcome to our family."

"Thank you." For some reason, tears sprung to her eyes and Evangeline fought not to cry. "I must be overly tired. I am sincerely delighted to be here."

Mariel Maclean gave her a warm smile and introduced her to Ian Maclean, who was but a year younger than Camren and then Adele, their sister, who looked to be just a bit older.

"Of course, you must meet my brother and his wife." Mariel motioned to an older man and woman who were a bit more restrained in their welcome. But the woman did smile warmly at her.

Finally, they made their way into the house and, once again, Evangeline wanted to kick her husband at his lack of proper description of his home. The room they entered and referred to as a great room, was indeed that. The vast open space with whitewashed walls was grand. There were four long tables set for a meal. At the front was a table on a high board that was almost as long. There were two hearths, each one with seating areas that would comfortably host six or more. From wooden rafters hung huge candelabras and along the walls, the gazes of men and women depicted on the portraits followed their entrance.

The smell of fresh flowers from the vases on the tables reminded her of home and the garden back in London.

"Once we feed you, I imagine you'll want to rest for a bit," Mariel said as they sat at the nearest table. "I was able to put off anyone coming to visit for a day. A betrothal party will be thrown to celebrate in a couple days of course."

"That is very kind of you, but not necessary," Evangeline said and realized her mistake when Adele chuckled and exchanged a look with Mariel.

Camren's mother's eyes twinkled with mirth. "It is tradition. Camren is laird and, therefore, the clan expects to be part of each important occasion of his life. The entire clan and neighboring ones are to be invited for the wedding."

Evangeline looked for Camren, who'd left her side and wandered away. He, Gideon and Daniel were at the farthest hearth speaking with his brother, Ian. Their voices were low.

"Is Ian's wife not here?"

"Oh, she is," Mariel said with a grin. "She is heavy with child and cannot be about right now. We expect the babe to be born within days."

"I would love to meet her."

"Of course," Adele said, motioning for a maid who walked up and set food down on the closest table. She looked to the high board. "We don't use that table except when entertaining other lairds or such. Most of the time we eat at this table."

An angry Lucille was carried past to where Evangeline assumed was the kitchen. "My cat is very spoiled. Perhaps I should see about the feline."

"Don't worry," Adele said with an indulgent look toward where Lucille was taken. "Our housekeeper adores cats and will ensure she is well. Wait until you meet Alastair, her stately cat, who considers itself above all humans."

Relieved but still a bit worried, Evangeline decided she was much too exhausted to look after Lucille at the moment. "I do need to rest for a bit."

"Eat first and I will show you to your room." Camren's mother poured something into cups. "It's a bit of honeyed mead."

The food was quite delicious and rich. Despite her being tired, she ate heartily, feeling comfortable in the company of the women present. She bit her tongue when wanting to ask where Camren would be sleeping, recalling she was to pretend to be his fiancée and not wife.

"How long before our wedding?" she asked, glancing toward Camren who now ate across the table from her.

He pressed his lips together and Evangeline narrowed her eyes. Her husband was enjoying this too much.

"I would say a fortnight. Two weeks should be enough time. Or we can wait longer if you wish," Mariel commented. "If you'd like to wait for your family to come."

"No," both she and Camren said at the same time.

Camren cleared his throat and lowered his voiced. "Mother, the sooner the better. You see, Evangeline and I precipitated our relationship further than we should have."

At Evangeline's gasp, everyone at the table began to laugh.

"I see," her mother said, giving her son a stern look that was lightened by the chuckle that followed. "I am not surprised."

This time, Evangeline hid her face in her hands. Adele nudged her. "What mother means is you are so very beautiful. We understand why Camren would have such a hard time resisting."

"In that case, the wedding will be in two weeks," Mariel announced.

When Camren gave her an amused look, Evangeline glared at him. "You are incorrigible. I am not sure what to say."

Adele patted her hand. "Ian's wife was expecting their first when they married. Quite the scandal." Everyone laughed again and

Evangeline was immediately in love with the family. They were accepting and forward-thinking.

She wondered how they'd react to the story of her leg injury. Of course, Evangeline had no plans to ever speak of it. She and Camren had not come up with an explanation for her limp.

"May I have a quick word with you," Evangeline said to Camren once they finished their meal.

Once he helped her to stand, they went to the far side of the room. She glanced up at him. "What will we say when they ask about my leg?"

"I will leave that up to you. Perhaps a carriage accident? Although my family is accepting and I doubt you will be judged, I also understand if you prefer not to share all the details."

"I will leave it at a carriage accident. In case you are asked, I want to be sure we both say the same thing."

He nodded and pressed a kiss to her forehead in the most endearing manner. "Thank you for coming home with me. I am sure you will be happy. I will ensure it."

Once again, she felt like crying and sniffed. "I adore your family already." She wiped her eyes. "Goodness, I need to sleep. I am so very tired."

Camren hugged her and guided her back to the table. "Evangeline is about to fall from exhaustion."

"Poor dear." Mariel stood. "Come." Adele and Mariel flanked Evangeline and guided her up the stairs to a bedroom that was twice the size of hers in London. A large four-poster bed drew her attention and she let out a sigh. "Thank you both so much. I feel so very welcome."

Molly, her maid, entered, looking refreshed, which made Evangeline wonder how it was possible.

"Rest. You are home now, dear." Mariel hugged her, and she and Adele left.

"Why do you look so spry?" Evangeline asked Molly. "I am barely able to keep my eyes open."

"I slept most of the time," Molly replied with a grin. "I'm so excited to be here. My mother's family lives nearby."

No sooner than she climbed into bed did Evangeline fall into a deep slumber. Not even her husband joining her roused her from the depths of sleep.

CHAPTER SEVENTEEN

E VEN AFTER A full night's sleep, Evangeline woke with a stiff back and aching shoulders. When she stretched, it felt so good that she smiled. Then upon sensing someone watching, she turned to find Camren in bed with her.

"What are you doing here? Your mother will find out," she hissed at him, immediately looking around as if expecting someone to walk in any minute and finding them.

"Shhh," Camren said, pulling her against him. "If we're very quiet, no one will know I'm here." His warm lips pressed against the sensitive spot just beneath her jaw and of their own volition, her eyes closed.

One of his hands was already inching up her thigh to pull her against his arousal. He was more than ready, and she couldn't help the shivers of anticipation.

"We really… shouldn't," she protested weakly. "Someone will… oh." He prodded at her entrance, sending a lightning bolt of heat to her very core.

When she attempted to speak again, Camren covered her mouth with his and thrust his tongue in.

Evangeline threw one leg over his hip to allow him easier entrance. He drove in smoothly and she let out a loud moan. The kiss grew intense, his mouth suckling her tongue and then inviting her to do the same.

He pushed in and pulled out in a smooth, concise rhythm that she'd learned to associate with him. Camren didn't hurry when making love. He took time to ensure she was completely sated before allowing himself release.

"Yes," Evangeline whispered, wrapping her arms around him and matching his movements. He trembled with restraint, which she found so very erotic.

He pulled out and placed his lips to her ear. "Turn around." When she did, he positioned her so that her bottom was even with his sex and he entered her while his fingers played between her legs.

"Ahhh!" Evangeline caught herself and pushed her face against the pillow so she could muffle her cries of release.

Every inch of her body stiffened with anticipation of what was to come and, seconds later, she floated from invisible heights.

Camren continued to drive in and out of her, nearing his peak. Evangeline tried to move, but her body was limp, and her muscles refused to comply. And so, instead, she mewled into the bed coverings as her husband continued moving.

When he found release, Evangeline had managed to once again shatter a second time.

Camren pulled her against him, her back to his chest and bit down on her throat, marking her as his, the act so primal that she dissolved in want. "Please…"

"Hold still, love." He pleasured her with his talented fingers, not stopping until she came with so much force that stars formed behind her eyes. Evangeline finally went limp, unable to fathom how it was possible for him to know her body so well.

Moments later, she turned in his arms. "You should leave. Someone will come. Probably heard us."

Camren chuckled. "The idea of being found out thrilled you, didn't it? Three times, Evangeline, really?" His teasing made her blush.

"Stop it and go now."

"Not until you admit it's true. You are a thrill seeker."

"Very well, perhaps it helped, but I find you extraordinarily attractive and that alone creates great love-making." She shoved at him, but he didn't budge. "Camren, you have to sneak out."

Finally, after she pushed him again, he slid from the bed and stretched. "I need to find something to wear." He walked to the wardrobe.

"Is this your room?" Evangeline sat up and gawked at him. "Why am I in your room?"

He grinned at her. "My family knows we are here together."

His chuckles washed over her as she fell back into the bed. Evangeline couldn't help but laugh as well. "You tricked me."

WHEN THEY DESCENDED the stairs, Evangeline was shocked to see how many people had gathered in the great room. Almost every seat was filled with people who stopped midsentence or midbite to watch them walk in.

Her stomach dipped at so many strangers at once. She swallowed when she took a step which would make her limp noticeable.

Camren must have felt her tense because he squeezed her hand. Then at once, the people gathered called out something in Gaelic that was followed by a response. It was repeated several times.

"What are they saying?" Evangeline asked.

"A congratulations of sorts," Camren replied and held both hands up to quiet the crowd.

"I will speak in English so my betrothed will understand," he started and looked to her. "Much appreciation for welcoming me back. Thankfully, I returned upright."

There was laughter at his comment. Once again, those gathered quieted. "I present Evangeline Prescott, soon to be called Lady Maclean." He motioned to her and there were sounds of appreciation. Some sounded a bit raunchy and were followed by laughter.

Camren leaned to her. "I am afraid Scots can be a bit uncivilized at times. But they mean well."

"It's refreshing," Evangeline replied, meaning it. She bowed her head to the crowd. "Thank you, I think."

There was more laughter. Her heart swelled at seeing the respect and gladness the people had toward her husband. In that instant, she understood why he owed them a wedding.

They did not sit at the high board, but went to the same table she'd eaten at the night before. A young girl rushed to her with a fistful of limp flowers and Evangeline reached to get them. She gave the girl a hug and was repaid with a wide grin.

Before she could sit, several other young girls followed suit, hoping to get a hug. Evangeline was falling in love with the children before breakfast.

Once seated, Adele gave her a warm smile. "They are astonished at your beauty. Your hair is so bright, everyone is remarking on it."

"I will have to learn Gaelic. I am afraid it is not a language I studied. But I am a quick learner and hope to pick it up."

Camren's mother nodded. "It will be best that you do. However, right now, we must focus on the wedding. It is most important, especially given my son refuses to be away from you."

When the others at the table chuckled, Evangeline could feel her face heat up. "I would be grateful. I brought a gown and veil, as well."

"I can't wait to see them," Adele exclaimed.

There was a hush and every eye turned to the doorway. A beautiful brunette stood in the center with fists on her hips, her extended belly protruding as she fired a glare toward the table where the family sat. "I'm hungry," she snapped and waddled to the table.

"Of course, you are, dear," Camren's mother and sister hurried to the woman and helped her to sit.

The brunette's eyes snapped to Evangeline. "You must be the beautiful Sassenach. I'm Sencha, that brute's wife." She pointed at Ian who looked to his mother as if not sure what he should do.

"Shouldn't you be in bed?" Ian finally asked.

"If she can walk, then no. It will help the babe come faster for her to be about," Mariel replied. "Once you eat, we will walk in the garden."

Sencha smiled widely at her mother-in-law. "That sounds delightful."

"It is very nice to meet you," Evangeline finally said. "I would like to join you for a walk. I love gardens. I hope to bring my cat out there."

"A cat?" Sencha asked, her brown eyes rounding. "You brought at cat from England?"

"Yes," Evangeline replied, not sure why it was so strange. "My cat is quite dear to me."

"I will also join you," Adele said. "The men will go about their things and we shall walk and entertain Sencha."

"No. No," Sencha said, motioning to Evangeline. "We have a wedding to plan. Ian says it must be done with haste." Her gaze moved toward Evangeline's flat stomach.

Once again, she blushed. But this time, she pushed embarrassment away. The Scottish were definitely very different from the English.

THE GARDEN WAS a delightful mixture of flowers, short bushes and vegetables. There were fruit trees that Evangeline had never seen and an enormous food garden near the kitchens.

Evangeline stopped and looked up at a tree. "What sort of fruit is this?"

Mariel joined her. "This is a plum tree. We have many. Also, there are a few pears, as well. Did you have a garden back at home?"

"I lived in the center of London, but we still had a lavish garden. Not as large as this, but it is beautiful. Mother planted mostly flowers, but our cook and housekeeper, Martha, has a small patch where she plants vegetables. We did have a pair of pear trees."

"I cannot wait for the fruit to ripen so we can make tarts," Mariel said, looking up at the fruit. "Soon."

They continued walking, the women pointing out areas informing Evangeline of what was housed where. They walked just outside the gates which gave them a clear view of the surrounding lands. On a hill to the left, another manor stood. Evangeline was informed it belonged to a relative, an uncle of Camren's who was part of Clan Maclean. Directly forward, a winding road led to a village. People mingled about what looked to be a square. To the right of the village was a large field and further from there sat a farm. Sheep grazed on hills that grew lush, green grasses.

"This is certainly very different from London," Evangeline said almost to herself. "I cannot possibly describe the beauty in the letters I will write my mother and friend."

"I felt the same way upon arriving," Mariel said. "Although I am Scottish, I grew up in the Lowlands, near Edinburgh, which is closer to what I imagine London is."

Adele pointed past the other keep. "There is a second village a bit farther. It is smaller than the one down there."

They returned to the house. Evangeline searched for a put-out Lucille. Although the cat seemed quite at home next to the hearth, it refused to look at her.

After spending a few moments with her cat, Evangeline joined the women in a sitting room on the second level of the keep and spent several hours planning the wedding.

She'd hoped to take time to write letters, but time passed quickly, and she could barely stay awake through the long feasting that evening.

"Go to bed. I will follow you in a few moments. I have to speak to my brother for a few moments," Camren told her. Standing and holding out his hand, he walked her to the bottom of the stairs.

CAMREN ENTERED WHAT used to be his father's study. His brother, Ian, and Gideon joined him. Ian poured whisky into three glasses and they each took one.

"Gideon told me what happened," Ian said. "I am sure the message has reached Cowan."

Camren took a long draw. "I dislike resorting to violence, but they brought us to it."

"We acquired good business partners in England. However, with the agreements being so new, expectations must be met or else we can lose them," Gideon said.

The men were deep in thought for a moment until Ian gave Camren a long look. "You are getting married. Have you spoken to Madeline yet?"

He shook his head. "No, she was most put out yesterday. I didn't have time today. I will speak with her. I do not wish her to do something rash."

"A woman scorned is dangerous," Gideon remarked.

Ian shrugged. "It may also be prudent that you tell Evangeline about your relationship. Although by the way the two were glaring at each other upon your arrival, I would guess she suspects."

"It is a first. Usually it is me who has such entanglements." Gideon laughed and poured a second whisky.

Camren held out his glass for more, as well. "Speaking of which, I am told Rose plans to travel here. Do you plan to court her? If so, perhaps you should start cutting ties with Irene... and Merida."

"You may also wish to inform Glenda, the butcher's daughter. She is quite handy with the carving knife," Ian added.

Gideon sank into a chair. "I do have to ensure to clear things up before Rose arrives." His face brightened. "Or perhaps I'll wait and see. It could be each farewell could take a wee bit of time."

"In other words, you will be running for your life, my friend," Camren said. "I look forward to being entertained."

"Then you are not serious about this woman, Rose?" Ian asked, giving Gideon a pointed look.

Gideon flushed and looked into his glass. "If I am, there is not much I can do. She lives in England and I live here in Scotland. We didn't have time to get to know each other well. She did make me promise to return."

"You're in love," Ian said matter-of-factly. "Interesting."

An hour later, a bit unsteady after too many whiskies, Camren headed to seek his bed.

"We should talk." Madeline appeared from the shadows. "Is it true? You are to marry her? An Englishwoman?" Disdain dripped from each word. "What about me? Us?"

Camren tried to sober up enough to speak clearly, but he realized it was not the time for the discussion.

"I've missed you." Madeline moved closer and wrapped her arms around his neck. "Didn't you think of me?"

"I have to think of you?" He stumbled to make sense. "I had to not think of you."

She brought him down for a kiss and the moment their lips touched, he pushed away. "No. I can't. You aren't my wife."

"Wife? You are not married yet," Madeline hissed. "We can still enjoy each other. Just one more night."

Camren straightened. "I'm late to sleep. We can speak tomorrow."

When he continued toward his bedchamber, Evangeline's maid stood at the entrance to the kitchen. The young woman curtsied and hurried away.

CHAPTER EIGHTEEN

WHEN CAMREN WOKE, Evangeline looming over him startled him. His eyes widened and then narrowed. "Good morning?"

She knew he'd drank too much the night before and that morning, her maid informed her promptly of a woman coming on to him before he rebuffed her and came to bed. However, it was nice to have a little secret to hold over him and enjoy it for a few moments.

"Who did you kiss last night?"

He scowled. "You. I think."

"Really?" She pretended to be annoyed. "In your sleep you were mumbling about kissing someone, but the name was not mine."

It was comical when he tried to sit up. But she did not budge, her hands firmly planted on both sides of his shoulders. The man was strong and could have easily pushed her aside. However, he was intelligent enough to know it wouldn't be wise.

"If you're speaking of my encounter with Madeline. She kissed me."

Evangeline huffed. "Does it matter who kisses whom? It is still a kiss."

After yawning and a few lip smacks, as if he were relaxed, he lifted up, taking her with him and pulled her against his chest. "I will speak to her today. I never mentioned her to you because there were only physical interactions between me and her."

Interested, Evangeline peered up at him. "I like the way you handle things."

"How so?" he scowled.

"You don't lie or make excuses for what happened. Matter-of-fact is how I would describe it."

"Would you like to be present when I speak to her?"

"Absolutely," Evangeline said, pushing away and sliding from the bed. "Molly says you told her I was your wife."

"The maid missed very little," he mumbled.

Evangeline pressed her lips together to keep from smiling. "Yes, that's true, for which I'm glad."

"I was going to tell you," Camren said while pulling on his clothes.

AFTER FIRST MEAL, Evangeline went to search out Lucille. Just as she walked out to the garden carrying the purring cat, she caught sight of Madeline. The woman saw her as well and visibly bristled.

Evangeline placed Lucille down, the cat trotting to find a place to explore. When she straightened, she pinned Madeline with a look. "Last night will be the last time you approach my husband. Never again. Am I understood?" She maintained direct eye contact until Madeline looked away.

"There must be a reason he is marrying you," the woman said in a heavy brogue. "He and I have been lovers for months. Never once has he looked at another woman."

"There is a difference between being lovers and being betrothed. He and I will marry soon, the circumstances do not matter."

Madeline gave a one-shouldered shrug. "Don't be too sure he won't come to my bed once the novelty of an Englishwoman wears off."

"I would say it's the other way around. You are who he grew tired of." Evangeline walked away, hating her limp in that moment. But at the same time, she worried as she'd lost sight of Lucille. She ducked behind bushes and whispered, "Lucille. Come."

"Madeline," a man's voice called out and Evangeline stopped and watched as a husky man approached Madeline.

The woman seemed surprised to see him. "Ronan, what are you doing here?"

By his attire, he was a tradesman of sorts. The well-honed body told Evangeline that his work entailed physical strength. "I came to say goodbye."

As much as Evangeline didn't wish to eavesdrop, she didn't dare leave, as Lucille emerged from a flowering bush and decided to plop down next to the man's boot.

"Where are you going?" Madeline neared the man, no longer seeming to remember Evangeline's presence. She placed a hand on the man's arm. "Tell me where."

"I am returning to Uist. There is no need to remain here. You've made a new life for yourself just like you planned, and it doesn't include me."

Evangeline held her breath. Had Madeline moved there with this man Ronan and then taken up with Camren?

"I am so very sorry for everything, Ronan." Madeline looked like she was about to cry. Evangeline stared at Lucille, willing the feline to come to her. The cat decided, instead, it was the perfect time to groom.

If she moved now, Madeline would see her. So she remained frozen slightly behind a tall plant.

"I know you are," Ronan replied and reached to touch Madeline's face. "I still love you, but I must do what is best for me."

The man turned and walked away. With shoulders slumped, Madeline looked on. Both had their backs to Evangeline now, so she motioned to Lucille who gave her a bland look.

Just then, Madeline called out Ronan's name. She raced to the man and wrapped her arms around his chest. They were too far for Evangeline to hear what was said, but it seemed as if the woman had a change of heart.

"Leave with him," Evangeline whispered and then yelped when someone touched her shoulder.

"Who are you speaking to?" Camren came up behind her.

"No one," Evangeline replied too quickly, turning to face him. "Where did you come from?"

He pointed to a gate. "I was out with the guards and spotted your pastel gown."

"My dresses are quite different. I will have to get more serviceable ones made."

"What is going on?" He looked to where Madeline and Ronan stood talking.

The couple was no longer hugging. But they continued in deep conversation. Evangeline motioned to Lucille, who finally deemed it time to pad closer. "I brought Lucille out, saw her. I told her that she was not to go anywhere near you. Then the man there showed up, told her he was leaving. She chased after him. They hugged and now I think she may be going with him."

Camren looked from Lucille to the couple and lastly to her. "I hope so. He is a good man."

"She left him for you," Evangeline pointed out. "How could you do it, knowing he is..."

"I didn't know about him until much later." Camren took her hand.

Evangeline reached down to pick up her cat who at once began purring. "I am still not sure how I feel about her."

"Lucille? She's a good cat, I'm sure."

"Not the cat..."

Camren pressed a swift kiss to her lips. "Aren't you famished?"

"We just ate."

His lips curved. "It's been hours."

"I am going inside."

"Walk with me." Camren tugged her hand. "I wish to spend some time alone."

Evangeline walked with him around the building and down a light slope to a grassy area facing the shore. She stopped in her tracks at seeing a blanket spread on the ground. Next to it was a basket with bread and fruit.

"A picnic…" she blinked and looked to Camren. "For me?"

"For us," Camren said, pulling her to sit on the blanket with him.

"How delightful." Evangeline smiled broadly. "This is a first for me. I've picnicked with my family, but never a romantic one." She lowered to the blanket and arranged her skirts to the side after releasing Lucille who immediately decided the blanket was the perfect place to nap.

Camren lowered to one knee. "I have something to tell you." He took her hand and pierced her with a straight look. "I discovered something while speaking to my brother and Gideon last night."

The sense of her stomach falling made her flinch. "What happened?" she asked in a tiny voice.

"I am in love with you." The green specks in his hazel gaze darkened. "I think I fell in love with you the first moment I saw you sitting in a carriage at Hyde Park."

Evangeline swallowed. "I didn't think you noticed me."

"A man would have to be blind not to."

"But what happened last night that brought this realization?"

He chuckled. "Ian was informing Gideon of his way with woman and pointed out some things that made me think. I realized that I never wish to be with anyone else but you. I am in love with you, Evangeline Prescott Maclean and look forward to our life together."

In that moment, it was as if every emotion she'd held inside since her fall from grace loosened. Evangeline covered her face with both hands and began sobbing.

"Th-that… is s-so be-beauti-f-ful," she stammered. "I-I love…" she couldn't speak as the overwhelming waves of emotions swept her away.

Every so often, the reason for why something had to happen becomes clear and Evangeline knew that if not for her foolish actions, she would have never married Camren Maclean. Her perfect match.

Placing his fingers under her chin, he lifted her wet face. "Why are you so upset?"

"I'm not upset," she managed. "I'm happy." She pointed at what was surely a blotchy face. "I am so very h-happy."

Camren laughed and kissed her. "In that case, I am glad."

"I love you, too," Evangeline said when the kissed ended. "Very much."

CHAPTER NINETEEN

A Month Later

As AFTERNOON FELL over the keep, a restlessness she'd felt for days returned. There was plenty to do in her new home. Camren's mother had abdicated many of the duties of overseeing the house to her, preferring to advise instead of doing. The woman spent most of her time in the garden or helping care for Ian's newborn son, the first grandchild.

The wedding feast and celebration had lasted for three entire days. Now, she and Camren had many social obligations as they'd received countless invitations to sup with nearby lairds. They also planned a trip the visit the larger Maclean Clan off the coast on the Isle of Mull.

She'd visited the local village on several occasions with Adele, who loved greeting the people there and shopping for different things at the square. They'd even enjoyed a delightful meal at the tavern. The owner, a ruggedly handsome man, had refused to charge for their meals.

So far, the entire move to Scotland had proved a good change. Her husband was handsome and attentive, she got along well with his family and other than learning Gaelic, which she'd already picked up a few phrases, there was nothing to complain about.

Admittedly, she missed London, but couldn't claim to miss the social events, as she'd not attended hardly any in years. However, she did wake some mornings wishing to find Martha in the kitchen to share a cup of tea with. Reading letters from her mother was not a replacement for seeing her daily.

"Lady Maclean," Molly said from behind her. "Would you like me to gather some flowers for your sitting area?"

"No, thank you, Molly. I plan do so myself later today. Or perhaps tomorrow." She looked over her shoulder at the maid who pulled a gown out and hung it on the wardrobe door. "What is that for?"

"Laird and Lady MacLachlan's visit," Molly replied. "They are to be here for last meal. I was told by the housekeeper to ensure you wore something fashionable to outshine everyone, as the laird's mother does not care for the woman."

"Ah, yes, I remember now." Evangeline giggled. "The woman was not at all friendly at the wedding. I suppose there must be something that happened in the past between them."

The maid shrugged. "Your mother said to make sure to remind you to wear lilac when you wish to look your best."

At the words, her throat constricted. "She did love that color on me."

Evangeline turned away to peer out again so Molly would not see that tears stung and threatened to spill.

In the distance, a large carriage appeared, a second one behind. The visitors were traveling at a slow speed, not seeming to rush to arrive.

"They arrive." Evangeline went to the mirror. Currently, she wore a cream dress. It was cut simply with a square collar and short, bell-shaped sleeves. There was little in the way of adornment which made the pearl buttons and peeking of lace around the waist stand out.

Although not elaborate, Evangeline knew the dress enhanced her skin tone and brought out the green in her eyes. The cut was flattering as well, showcasing her small waist.

There wasn't anything to do as her hair was styled and her skin was flushed from the fresh air that blew in through the window.

When she descended the stairs, Camren, Ian and their mother were already heading to the door.

"Who is it?" Mariel asked.

"I don't know, Mother," Camren said and turned to see that Evangeline approached. He held out his hand to her. "We are about to greet whoever it is that comes."

The Highland tradition of greeting was warm and welcoming. Evangeline liked it. Although at times, she felt strange standing at the front door as carriages pulled up.

"I do not recognize the emblem," Adele called out from the second-story window. She peered out to the gates, with one hand over her eyes. "Not local."

Mariel looked up. "Come down here at once and stop gawking out the window like a village laundress."

Evangeline giggled and Mariel shook her head. "She should be in her own home. Why is she here?"

"She wanted to spend time with the babe," Ian replied.

Everyone straightened as the carriages pulled into the courtyard. Then Evangeline grabbed Camren's hand. "It's my parents." Her eyes rounded as she caught sight of her mother waving.

Across from her mother in the other window, Rose peered out, her gaze taking in the large keep. Then she looked to Evangeline and blew a kiss.

"THIS IS AMAZING," Rose exclaimed and threaded her arm around Evangeline's. They walked through the garden to the slope where Camren had planned their picnic. Evangeline wanted to share the experience with her friend.

"Magical, isn't it?" Evangeline replied. "I had no idea. Camren never described his home to me. I suppose with everything that was happening, we never had the opportunity to discuss it. The grandeur of the house, if one could call it that, overwhelms me."

"I'd say it's a castle," Rose interjected. "You, my friend, live in a castle."

They continued on for a few steps, Evangeline sliding a look to a nearby field where Gideon, Camren and several men practiced with swords. She was sure it was Gideon's idea, a way of showing off to Rose.

"Have you and he spoken yet? I am sure he will try to convince you to stay longer."

A soft blush colored Rose's cheek. "We have not been alone, no." She looked to where the men were. "Do you really think he is attracted to me?"

"Of course, he is. You should have seen how happy he was when finding out you came with my parents.

"Perhaps we will speak. I wouldn't mind staying with you a bit longer. I miss you terribly."

"I miss you, as well." Evangeline sighed happily. For now, everything was perfect.

"I am blessed that our parents are so compatible. Even now, the four went to visit Laird MacLachlan so father can see his horses."

"What of the other brother," Rose asked. "Have you met the youngest yet?"

Evangeline shook her head. "I like Ian and from what I hear, the youngest is the wildling of the three. He sails the seas and prefers the life of a nomad. His reputation of a privateer is bordering on that of a pirate. I do look forward to meeting him. Mariel says he comes home every summer and winter, so he should appear in the not too distant future."

"How romantic," Rose said, pretending to swoon. A brooding pirate in the family.

They continued their walk as Rose caught Evangeline up on what had happened back in London.

Once they returned inside, they went directly to the kitchens and asked for a bite to eat and tea, which Rose brought from England.

Chatting at a table in the great room, they were interrupted by a guard who entered and hesitated. "Lady Maclean, Mister Sutherland requested to speak to Miss Rose."

Evangeline smiled wide as Rose's eyes rounded. "He does? Very well. Escort her to him."

"What are you smiling about?" Adele neared and lowered to sit opposite her.

Camren's sister was like her own now. In the short time she'd been there, they'd grown quite close. "Gideon requested to speak to Rose."

"No." Adele jumped to her feet. "Why are we sitting here. Let's go see what happens." She grabbed Evangeline's hand and they hurried to the front door.

In the courtyard, near the gardens, they spotted Rose and Gideon. The large Scot towered over the petite Rose who reached for a red rose he held out for her.

"Oh, my," Adele whispered. "He is using her name to do something romantic."

Evangeline giggled. "What is he doing now?"

After accepting the flower, Rose took his arm and they walked further into the garden.

"I'd say," Adele said while craning her neck to get a better view, "we will have another wedding soon."

"Do you think he'll remain here?" Evangeline asked. "He owns a beautiful house in London. They may decide to live there."

The breeze blew across their faces and, for a moment, Evangeline inhaled the sweet smell from the garden's blooms. "I hope Rose doesn't demand to live in London. Although she is as close to her mother as I am to mine."

"Gideon will never leave Scotland. He is a Scot through and through." Adele gave a firm nod to make her point. "If they marry, Rose will have to accept it."

"Who's getting married?"

They turned to find Evangeline's mother and Mariel. Both peered past them to the garden.

Adele placed a finger over her lips. "Don't speak so loudly. Gideon and Rose are in there walking."

"Why are you spying?" Mariel asked, shaking her head. "Shame on you." The entire time she searched the garden, her eyes darting past them.

Evangeline's mother giggled. "I knew there was a reason Rose insisted on coming."

"She is my dear friend, Mother," Evangeline said. "What other reason would she have to insist on coming."

Her mother pointed to the garden. "It could be she wished to see a certain young man."

The four women went into the keep as it was getting time to prepare for last meal. Already clanspeople were gathering in the courtyard.

Mariel motioned for them to hurry. "We must freshen up and change into something more appropriate because tonight we have visitors and people from the village come to welcome your parents, Evangeline."

Evangeline took her mother's hand. "I wish you could stay here with me forever."

"Your father and I will visit regularly. His business is in London and I would never wish to be apart from him. Therefore, long visits will have to do."

They continued up the stairs and her mother pulled Evangeline to a stop. "Why aren't you limping as much?"

Evangeline shrugged. "I still limp, Mother."

"You walk differently though." Her mother frowned. "Interesting."

Although Evangeline didn't say anything, she knew why her gait was more concise. She was proud and happy and didn't feel the need to try to overcorrect her steps. It turned out that in walking with assuredness, the limp was not as noticeable.

LAST MEAL WAS loud, crowded and delightful. Evangeline had never seen her parents more animated than that night.

Her father obviously enjoyed the music, his head moving side to side and her mother sipped on honeyed mead, pronouncing it the best drink ever.

Platters piled high with food were carried around the room as servants refilled plates.

There was quail, goose and roasted boar on meat trays. Others carried trays with offerings of freshly roasted vegetables as well as breads and cheeses.

Unlike in polite society, rules for serving were disregarded and everyone took and ate without waiting for others at their tables to be served.

AFTER THE FEASTING, musicians played and people began dancing.

Suddenly, guards rushed into the room. The music stopped and a hush fell over the room.

Camren stood and stepped from the high board. He hurried to the door, followed by Ian.

Moments later, a tall, muscular, bearded man appeared. It had to be Cowan. Although the youngest of the brothers, he was broader. The brothers embraced, both Camren and Ian slapping the younger one's back.

Cowan stalked to the high board, his gaze on his mother. Then without preamble, he plucked her up and hugged her, turning in a circle. Adele was given the same treatment as everyone watched with smiles at the family reunion.

Unlike Camren and Ian, Cowan had dark brown hair and eyes. His gaze fell upon her for a moment.

He was a mixture of danger and sensuality. Evangeline understood why women would find him hard to resist. "Welcome to the family," he stated in a deep, throaty voice. "I hope you are settled and not allowing my brother too much freedom."

Evangeline smiled at Cowan, liking him. "Thank you. I will ensure he remains within reach at all times."

Cowan chuckled.

The music resumed.

The youngest sat next to Ian. Several maids hurried over to serve him, giving Evangeline the impression that they hoped to gain his favor.

Camren leaned to his brother. "We didn't expect you so soon."

There was a slight pause and the brothers exchanged some sort of silent conversation.

"I came to bring news. There was an unfortunate accident involving an Irish ship," Cowan said with a shrug. "Everyone perished."

Evangeline turned to Camren. "Everyone?"

"Did you not get my message, to spare…"

Cowan held up a hand. "It wasn't me." He smiled at his mother to reassure her. "This is a conversation best left for after we eat."

IT WAS LATE when Camren slipped into bed next to Evangeline. His hand immediately slipped under her nightgown, his fingers skimming over her skin and sending tingles of desire through her.

Sliding closer, Evangeline lifted her face and accepted the whisky-tinged kiss.

His lips pressed against hers and then trailed to her ear. "I want you so much."

"As do I," Evangeline replied, only to gasp as his arousal touched her thigh.

Within moments, they were lost in each other, no thoughts of the next day or the future. All that mattered in that moment was that they were in love and would spend many nights making love, sharing moments and learning that their marriage of happenstance did, indeed, make for a good life.

CLAN MACLEAN WOULD welcome the laird's first of three children that winter. The following spring, they would participate in the much-anticipated wedding between Gideon Sutherland and Rose Edwards, who would join those living at Keep Maclean.

The End

About the Author

Most days USA Today Bestseller Hildie McQueen can be found in her overly tight leggings and green hoodie, holding a cup of British black tea while stalking her hunky lawn guy. Author of Medieval Highlander and American Historical romance, she writes something every reader can enjoy.

Hildie's favorite past-times are reader conventions, traveling, shopping and reading.

She resides in beautiful small town Georgia with her super-hero husband Kurt and three little doggies.

Visit her website at www.hildiemcqueen.com
Facebook: HildieMcQueen
Twitter: @HildieMcQueen
Instagram: hildiemcqueenwriter

Manufactured by Amazon.ca
Bolton, ON